"It's only for one night. The next day we say our goodbyes and leave."

"Together," Lucas put in.

"Of course together! We'll travel home and that will be that. It's just twenty-four hours. Midnight to midnight, then we'll go our separate ways. We need never see each other again."

Lucas looked thoughtful. "There's just one thing that puzzles me. I don't understand why, when you've gone to all this trouble arranging a date and telling your parents, you're still so insistent on keeping things strictly business. Why not make it for real? Then we could have some fun."

"Fun?" Georgia spluttered indignantly. "And I suppose by fun you mean—"

"I mean this," Lucas drawled softly and, leaning forward, kissed her right on the mouth.

KATE WALKER was born in Nottinghamshire, but as she grew up in Yorkshire she has always felt that her roots were there. She met her husband at university and she originally worked as a children's librarian, but after the birth of her son she returned to her old childhood love of writing. When she's not working, she divides her time between her family, their three cats and her interests of embroidery, antiques, film and theater, and, of course, reading.

You are invited to celebrate two of the most talked about weddings of the decade—lavish marriages where the cream of society gathers in dazzling international settings.

SOCIETY WEDDINGS

Two original short stories in one volume:
Promised to the Sheikh by Sharon Kendrick
The Duke's Secret Wife by Kate Walker
On sale August, Harlequin Presents #2268

Books by Kate Walker

HARLEQUIN PRESENTS®
2160—RAFAEL'S LOVE-CHILD

Hers for a Night

KATE WALKER

THE MILLIONAIRES

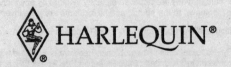

HARLEQUIN®

TORONTO • NEW YORK • LONDON
AMSTERDAM • PARIS • SYDNEY • HAMBURG
STOCKHOLM • ATHENS • TOKYO • MILAN • MADRID
PRAGUE • WARSAW • BUDAPEST • AUCKLAND

ISBN 0-373-80517-9

HERS FOR A NIGHT

First North American Publication 2002.

Copyright © 1996 by Kate Walker.

Visit us at www.eHarlequin.com

Printed in U.S.A.

CHAPTER ONE

'AND now, ladies and gentlemen, we come to the high spot of the evening—the moment I'm sure you've all been waiting for!'

The woman standing on the stage at the far end of the large, luxurious dining room banged her gavel on the table in front of her in order to gain attention, even though it was obvious that she had no need to do so. Every head in the crowd before her was already turned in her direction, the buzz of conversation fading to a silence that was somehow electric with a new and expectant excitement.

'Here we go,' Georgia muttered to herself, sitting upright in her chair and running a hand over her sleek copper-coloured hair before adjusting the short skirt of her mint-green silk suit, infected by the tension as much as everyone else.

This was what she had come here for. This was the reason—the only reason—she had paid the exorbitant ticket price and endured an indifferent meal, a less than enjoyable cabaret.

'Lot twenty-five in our charity auction. A very special offer indeed for the connoisseur. A must for any lady with discerning taste and a bank balance to match! I'm sure that more than one of you would be willing to spend any amount to purchase the services—' the elegant brunette rolled her eyes dramatically '—of this particular man for a day. Ladies and gentlemen, our star attraction—Mr Lucas Mallory!'

Star attraction indeed, Georgia thought to herself, and from the look of him this man knew it only too well.

Others before him had ambled down the catwalk in the centre of the room with an embarrassed, almost shamefaced air, as if they couldn't quite believe their own behaviour in appearing in a 'slave auction' like this. Some had attempted a more confident swagger, but had only succeeded in looking cocksure and rather silly, and others had been so painfully ill at ease that Georgia had winced inwardly in empathic embarrassment.

In contrast to such displays, Lucas Mallory strolled out into the glare of the spotlight with the easy, unruffled confidence of a man born to public favour and acclaim.

Everything about him, his firmly upright carriage, the assured lift of his chin, the measured, hunting-cat grace with which he moved, declared that he was sure of his welcome. Without a word having to be spoken he made it plain that he had never doubted for a moment what his reception would be like.

And he was right, of course. The ripple of applause that greeted his appearance swelled in volume as he strolled down the catwalk, growing to a thunderous roar when he came to a halt at the end. From his higher position, he surveyed the crowded room with leisurely nonchalance, a faint smile curving the corners of his beautifully shaped mouth and one dark eyebrow lifting in teasing challenge.

'Oh, very cool!' Georgia commented under her breath, her tone a blend of admiration and cynicism.

She was well aware of the fact that 'Cool' was reported to be Lucas Mallory's middle name. Nothing, it was said, but *nothing* fazed him in any way at all. Even the appalling crash that had almost claimed his life hadn't stirred a single shining hair on that handsome head.

'I'm sure that I don't have to tell you anything about Lucas Mallory.' On the stage, the auctioneer was warming to her theme. 'But for those of you who have been asleep for the past ten years or have just flown in from some far distant planet, let me say that the man before you was a World Champion racing driver. He won that accolade three times in succession, and might possibly have achieved a fourth win if it hadn't been for a run of bad luck that ended in his unexpectedly early retirement.'

Mr Cool hadn't liked that reference to his last, disastrous year in Grand Prix racing, Georgia reflected, seeing the tiny frown that creased the space between the straight, black brows. Clearly he would much rather have retired with yet another golden prize under his belt instead of being forced out of the competition by a string of problems and near disasters that made it seem as if his legendary luck had finally deserted him.

'But since then he has not been content to rest on his laurels. Instead, he has turned his attention to business, making a second fortune restoring and selling classic cars. So you can see that the woman who makes the winning bid tonight will be a lucky lady indeed. In fact, I can only bemoan the fact that I am not allowed to take part in this particular auction!'

The look the elegant brunette turned on Lucas Mallory could only be described as idolatrous, and Georgia felt a twist of deep cynicism as she saw the man at the end of the catwalk respond with a smile of megawatt brilliance that was clearly designed to have her, and every other woman in the room, melting into a warm pool at his feet.

That smile would get him anything, or anyone, as poor Kelly knew to her cost. For a couple of seconds the memory of her friend's distress blurred Georgia's hazel eyes and she had to shake her head firmly, sending her smooth mane of coppery coloured hair flying round her fine-boned face as she tried to drive the image from her mind.

She needed to concentrate on the plan that had brought her here tonight. Any thought of the callous way this man had behaved towards Kelly would only distract her from her purpose.

'But I'm sure you're anxious to get this part of the auction under way, so would anyone like to start the bidding?'

There was no shortage of volunteers, enthusiastic hands shooting up all around the room, but Georgia kept her own carefully manicured fingers firmly in her lap.

Steady, she warned herself, you don't want to look too eager.

That was not the impression she wanted to give at all. And besides, she could afford to wait, to let others increase the price until some of them were forced to drop out.

Lucas Mallory, too, seemed quite content to wait. He looked perfectly at ease even in the glare of the spotlight, hands pushed deep into the pockets of the perfectly tailored black trousers he wore with an equally elegant dinner jacket and immaculate white shirt.

But of course the spotlight was his natural habitat. He had hardly been out of it at any point during the past ten years. If the tabloid press hadn't been reporting his explosive success on the race track, then it had been the equally dramatic nature of his private life that had grabbed their interest.

The latter seemed to consist of a series of high-profile romances alternating with even more public break-ups—if 'romances' was the right word. Certainly his associations could never be described as relationships, none of them seeming to last long enough to do more than register on the public awareness before they were unceremoniously discarded and Lucas Mallory moved on to pastures new.

'Mallory's Moppets, we're known as.' Kelly's voice, shaking with bitterness, sounded inside her head. 'Or the Pit Stop Popsies. At least, the ones who get as far as a date are called that! There's another, even less flattering term that's used for the others—the ones like me. *I* barely had a chance to warm his sheets before he pushed me out the door. The proverbial one-night stand, that's me!'

'But why did you let it happen?' Georgia hadn't been able to hide her concern. 'Don't you have any more respect for yourself than that? Why didn't you just say no?'

'Say no!' her friend had echoed, rolling her eyes dramatically to emphasise just what she thought of that suggestion. 'Georgie, *no one* says no to Lucas Mallory, at least, no woman with red blood in her veins! He is *gorgeous*, the sexiest thing on two legs ever to walk this earth.'

And, in spite of feeling decidedly prejudiced against the man on the stage, Georgia had to admit that even 'gorgeous' was rather too restrained a term to describe someone like him. It implied the sort of conventional, almost pretty-boy looks that turned actors into movie stars. Lucas Mallory had features that were too strong, a bone-structure that was too harsh for such a glamorous appeal.

But when those strong-boned looks were teamed with hair that gleamed like polished jet and eyes that seemed, from this distance at least, to be almost equally dark, the impact this man had was like a blow to the soul. With square, powerful shoulders and a tall, leanly muscular frame that carried not even an ounce more in weight than when he had earned his living as a trained sportsman, then 'devastating' was probably far nearer the mark.

And he was absolutely perfect for what she wanted. He was all male, a modern day macho hero to his fingertips, and a self-made man as well. Oh, yes, her father would *love* Lucas Mallory.

'Any more? Would anyone like to raise…?'

Coming back to reality with a sense of shock, Georgia realised that she had been preoccupied for far longer than she had imagined. Already the bidding had slowed, the price having reached a total at which most of the interested parties had had to drop out. It was time to make a move.

'Going once…going twice.'

Georgia raised her hand. Her action caused a buzz of interest from the audience, who had believed the sale to be almost over.

'And a hundred,' she said firmly.

For a couple of minutes she had a battle on her hands. One determined woman on the other side of the room matched each increase she made, but then, reluctantly, she had to drop out, shaking her head regretfully.

'Sold!' The gavel came down on the table with a bang. 'Sold to Georgia Harding—you lucky thing! Please see Emily to pay, Georgie.'

Smiling to herself in satisfaction, Georgia got to her feet just as Lucas Mallory's dark eyes scanned the room, seeking out the person who had finally bought twenty-four hours of his time. As that alert, intent gaze rested on her for a moment some uncharacteristic imp of mischief urged her into action. Picking up her wine glass, she raised it in a mocking toast.

But the teasing gesture rebounded on her with a vengeance a moment later as the dark, sleek head inclined in sardonic acknowledgement of her salute. In the same instant, she saw the black eyes slide deliberately from the top of her shining red-gold head and down over her body to the smart Italian sandals whose slender, two-inch heels took her height to an impressive near six feet.

The coolly insolent survey was so blatantly sensual that she felt irritation prickle over her skin, a spark of anger flashing in her changeable eyes. From his behaviour, anyone would have thought that *she* was the slave and Lucas Mallory her lordly purchaser.

For a brief moment, gripped by blind fury, she was strongly tempted to declare that she had changed her mind. Let someone else put up with this man's arrogant assumption that any female must be putty in his hands!

But then common sense reasserted itself. After all, he was *perfect*, and once she had handed over her money he would be hers for the twenty-four hours that she needed him. After that, she would be only too pleased to see the back of him.

She was at the treasurer's table, signing her cheque with a firm, decisive hand, when some change in the atmosphere around her, an intuitive shiver of awareness over her skin, alerted her. She just had time to draw a deep, calming breath before the man who had come up behind her spoke.

'Miss Harding?'

It was a very attractive voice, low and pleasant. There was nothing in it to disturb her, but all the same she felt the tiny hairs at the nape of her neck lift in nervous response. Slowly she turned to face him, switching on a smile that was pure politeness, with no real warmth in it at all.

'Yes?'

Those eyes weren't actually black, she realised, seeing them properly for the first time. Instead, they were the deepest grey she had ever seen, dark and spectacular, like the rest of him. Her mind registered his impressive height and powerful build with an almost shocking force that rocked her mental balance, driving away the stern warnings Kelly had given her when she had told her friend what she had planned.

'I'm Lucas Mallory.'

Close up, the impact of that smile was even more lethal than it had been earlier. Then, its dazzling brilliance had been diluted by the distance between her seat and his position on the catwalk, but now there was no such safety device to weaken its power.

The hand he held out to her was lean and brown, its grip around her fingers disturbingly warm and strong.

Dear God, she was beginning to understand just how Kelly had felt, Georgia thought. Her head was swimming as she fought against the stunning sensual response that seared through her whole body. It was as if she had put her hand onto a live electric wire and been badly burned as a result.

She had to get a grip on herself! This was not at all how she had planned things would go.

'I know exactly who you are, Mr Mallory.'

The struggle to regain control of her wayward emotions made her voice even colder than she had planned, and she had to force herself to ease her hand gently from his grasp, fighting the impulse to snatch it away in panic. 'After all, I have just bought you.'

The dark eyes followed her gesture towards the cheque that now lay, fully signed, on the table beside a receipt for her donation. But when they swung back to her face she caught a disturbing gleam in their darkness.

'So the deal's been finalised—signed and sealed. I'm at your mercy. Yours to do with as you please.'

'Oh, really, Mr Mallory! Don't you think that's something of an exaggeration?'

Georgia's voice came and went embarrassingly, affected by the sudden, shockingly vivid image that slid into her mind. The thought of this powerful, intensely virile man at her mercy sent a shiver of reaction running down her spine.

'Not at all. When I agreed to take part in this auction, I knew that I'd end up as someone's "slave" at the end of it. I was well aware of the fact that once you'd paid there would be no getting out of it.'

'And would you want to get out of it? Is that what you're trying to say?'

'No way!'

All amusement had faded from those amazing eyes. Their dark intensity held her gaze transfixed, as if he was a powerful magnet and she the finest of needles, inevitably drawn to him.

'That thought never crossed my mind. I agreed to help, and I have no intention of going back on my word.'

His apparent sincerity was unexpected, making her wonder just why this particular charity was so important to him. Somehow she didn't connect Lucas Mallory, former Grand Prix champion and now wealthy businessman, with a fund to help premature babies. She might have expected he would give a donation, perhaps, but not this active participation.

But she didn't get a chance to question him about it, because the next moment that surprising seriousness had vanished from his eyes and the vivid smile was switched on once more.

'So now it's up to you. All you have to do is to tell me what you want from me, and I'm at your service. Believe me, it will be nothing but a pleasure to fulfil the desires of such a lovely lady.'

The man flirted as instinctively as he breathed! And in a way he had just given her some sort of explanation for his apparently charitable actions. After all, the whole point of this evening was that only the women present were allowed to bid for the male 'slaves'.

There was little doubt in Georgia's mind that Lucas,

whose sobriquet 'the fastest man on the track' didn't just refer to his racing exploits, had seen that he could turn this auction to his own advantage if the opportunity arose. And if it didn't arise naturally, then he would make sure it happened otherwise.

But not with this particular woman! If he thought that that amazing smile would have her melting helplessly at his feet, then he couldn't have been more wrong. If anything, it had the opposite effect, stiffening her spine and making her lift her chin in determined challenge. Kelly's face was clear in her mind, like some sort of mental shield with which to deflect the force of his practised charm.

'What I want is for you to stop flirting with me! This is a strictly business arrangement, and I'd prefer it if you kept it that way.'

Now she'd disconcerted him. She could see it in the way his face changed, all warmth fading from it. She could almost sense the swift adjustment in his thoughts as, mentally at least, he took a couple of steps away from her.

He hadn't expected that response, and it was obvious that he didn't like it. Clearly it rocked his macho pride to come up against a woman who was immune to his formerly infallible technique.

'Tell me,' Lucas Mallory murmured, in a tone that was so soft, so deceptively warm that for a moment she missed the warning in the tightness of the muscles around the strong jaw, 'are you usually this prickly with everyone or is this strictly personal?'

'I am *not* prickly!'

'No? Well, in that case I'd hate to meet you when you're in a bad mood.'

'My mood is my own business! And if it's not exactly welcoming, then perhaps you should remember that you're the one who imposed his company on me. I didn't invite you to join me!'

'Look, lady, I simply came over to introduce myself and find out what you wanted from me in return for your generous donation. I didn't know I had to wait for a formal introduction. After all, you're the one who made the first move by bidding for me. I had no intention of *imposing* on you in any way.'

Georgia flinched away from the lash of his sarcasm, knowing she had no defence against it. She was painfully aware of the possibility that, if she wasn't very careful, she could risk ruining all her plans by alienating him right from the start.

'Perhaps we'd better begin again.'

To her relief, Lucas followed her lead easily enough.

'Why don't I get us both a drink and then we can sit down and talk about it?'

'Fine. My table's over there.'

She had to forget how much she disliked men of Lucas Mallory's type, Georgia told herself firmly as she watched him make his way to the bar. After all, it was precisely because he had that sort of confident, macho lady-killer character that she had chosen him for this scheme in the first place.

She wasn't the only one who was watching, she noted. Even in the most crowded room, his imposing height and lean strength would mean that many eyes would be drawn to him. The forceful cast of his features under the silky dark hair inevitably made him the centre of much female attention.

But it wasn't just the female members of the audience who had turned their heads in Lucas's direction. The aura of confidence and complete self-assurance that seemed to emanate from him so easily made him an object of interest to men too. That interest was touched with a degree of envy, even from the few who were unaware of the full extent of his reputation and success. He would be a perfect match for her father in all ways.

'Fiver for them,' Lucas said quietly, making her jump as he placed two wine glasses on the table in front of her. She had watched him walk towards her, and yet now he seemed suddenly disturbingly close, towering over her in a way that she found slightly disturbing.

'I thought a penny was the usual rate,' she retorted, and saw his firm mouth curl up at the corners.

'In the everyday world, perhaps. But at this exclusive gathering I reckon the price must be commensurate with the exorbitant rates they charged for the tickets and the meal, so I worked on a five hundred percent increase.'

'That seems about right,' Georgia laughed. 'Why are you looking at me like that?'

He didn't answer in words but simply leaned forward and traced the outline of her curved upper lip with a gentle fingertip.

'Don't!'

Her head jerked back violently, as if the soft touch had been the burn of white-hot metal. Lucas, however, seemed unconcerned by the hostility of her response.

'You should smile more often, it changes your face completely,' he murmured. Then, as she deliberately clamped her mouth tight shut, erasing all traces of her earlier warmth, he pulled out the chair opposite and sat down, reaching for his wine glass. 'So what were you thinking about?'

Caught off balance, Georgia found that the words were out before she had time to form them fully in her mind.

'Oh, I was just realising how much you reminded me of my father.'

'Ah...' Lucas leaned back in his chair, dark eyes fixed on her face with an unnerving intensity. 'And is that what put that look on your face?'

'I—what look?'

'That "I would rather be anywhere else than here" expression.'

'Don't be silly!' Had she really given so much away? 'I mean, you know perfectly well why I'm here!'

'Do I?' The questioning lift to one dark eyebrow matched the sardonic note in his voice.

'Of course you do! After all, you're here for much the same reason.'

'I'm here to take part in an auction that's supposed to be a bit of fun, and by doing so help a charity that I—'

'Which is my aim too.'

'Really?'

The long, powerful body looked indolently relaxed in his chair, but the watchful darkness of his gaze, with his eyes slightly narrowed, and the restless tapping of one strong hand on the immaculate white linen of the table-cloth, told a very different story.

'Then why do I feel that there's some hidden agenda in all this?'

'Hidden agenda? Oh, really, Mr Mallory!'

'Lucas,' he corrected with a soft forcefulness that warned her he would allow for no prevarication.

'Lucas,' Georgia amended unwillingly.

His name sounded strange, alien on her tongue, and she had an unpleasant, unnerving feeling of things slipping out of her control.

This was not at all how she had planned that the evening would go. Not that she had really thought beyond the actual auction, she admitted to herself with uncomfortable honesty. She had been determined to be the highest bidder, to secure Lucas Mallory as her 'slave' for a day, but after that it had all been vague, to say the least.

One thing she had obviously not taken into account was the part that Lucas himself would play in all of it.

'There is no hidden agenda, no matter what crazy ideas your over-active imagination has come up with. Like you, I simply came here to support the charity, enjoy a meal and bid in the auction.'

'And that's the part that intrigues me,' Lucas inserted smoothly, throwing her off balance once more. 'It's obvious that you haven't entered into the light-hearted spirit of things like everyone else here. There seems to be a touch of...'

He paused, deliberately appearing to choose his words with infinite care.

'Of desperation about the way you're behaving.'

'Are you implying that the only way I can get a man is to buy one?'

Her voice was too sharp, too high-pitched, giving too much away.

'On the contrary, I'd have to be completely blind and all sorts of a fool to think any such thing. A woman with your looks would have no need of any such behaviour.'

'If you think flattery will win me over, you couldn't be more wrong!'

'It isn't flattery, and you know it.'

The indolent pose had been abandoned and he was leaning forward now. The restless movement of his hand had stilled, and one long finger was extended emphatically in order to reinforce his point.

'You're a spectacularly beautiful woman. You have style and money of your own. Your clothes would tell me that even if I hadn't just heard the outrageous amount you bid for my services. *My* services,' he repeated with a dangerous edge to his voice that made her heart jerk uncomfortably. 'You didn't even *look* at anyone else.'

The knots into which Georgia's nerves had twisted tightened painfully as she looked into his black, coldly probing eyes. How did he know that she had shown no interest in any of the other 'lots'? Had he been watching her before she had even been aware of him?

'Which begs the inevitable question—why me? What is it that I can offer you that others can't?'

'Well, it's perfectly simple.' Georgia snatched at the opening he had given her with a rush of relief. 'Really, Mr—Lucas—you've built this up out of all proportion. I have a rather special party coming up soon, and I need an escort. I don't happen to have a man in my life at the moment, so when I heard of the auction it seemed too good an opportunity to miss.'

It was half the truth after all, and it sounded perfectly reasonable—to her own ears at least. So why was he looking so sceptical, as if he didn't believe a word she had said?

'I mean, they were offering a man's services for twenty-four hours, and that was all that I needed. And as for the reasons why I chose you, I'm afraid you've rather flattered yourself on that score. There was nothing personal in it at all. I simply wanted to give as much as possible to the charity fund. After all, I can afford it. You just happened to be top of the bill.'

Deliberately she made the words sound cold and impersonal, insulting in their objectivity, and she knew that they had struck home as she saw his head go back sharply.

'It wasn't that I *chose* you. It could have been anyone.'

He didn't look convinced, damn him, but that was all she was prepared to say. Deep down, she had to admit that she was beginning to wish that she had chosen someone else, or had never had this idea in the first place.

'Any man would have done.'

'Is that a fact?' Lucas drawled, lacing the words with

silky cynicism. 'Well, you'll have to forgive me if I don't exactly believe you.'

'Don't exactly believe'! The arrogance of the man! She'd been warned strongly enough by Kelly, but until now she hadn't really believed that he could be quite as bad as he was painted. Now she saw he was all of that, and more.

'I realise that it must be difficult for you to believe that any woman would be able to resist your much-vaunted charms!' she flung at him, unable to keep her temper under control any longer. 'But, believe me, such a woman does exist! I want you to understand once and for all that any arrangement between us would have to be strictly business and nothing more.'

Georgia didn't know if it was devilish amusement or black anger that twisted Lucas's mouth sharply. She found herself unable to interpret his reaction as his dark head inclined in a gesture that might have been agreement, or something very different.

'Strictly business.'

'I want nothing more from you than your time and your—'

Hastily she caught herself up, painfully aware of the fact that she had been about to say 'your body'. She could just imagine the interpretation he might put on *that*.

'And your presence as my escort to the party. Is that clear?'

'Perfectly.' Lucas's tone matched hers in its clipped coldness—matched and outstripped it by a mile as it dripped icy condescension as he added, 'Though why you need to emphasise that point is beyond me.'

'What?' It was as if his words had been an actual, physical slap in the face, leaving her gasping with shock as he got to his feet with leisurely grace. 'I don't understand.'

'No?'

When he smiled like that, for all that the room was packed with people, Georgia suddenly felt as isolated and afraid as if she had been alone with him on some dark and deserted street.

Those black eyes held her hazel ones mockingly as he reached into the inner pocket of his elegant dinner jacket and pulled out a slip of white card.

'Then let me spell it out. You have no need at all to fear that our relationship will be anything other than the "strictly business" deal you're so determined to insist on. Because, you see, if I did want anything more personal—more intimate—then, believe me, you would be the last woman on earth I would choose.'

The casual way he tossed the card onto the table so that it fell just short of her hand was deliberately insulting in its arrogance. The insult was deepened by the offhand way he continued.

'My number's on there,' he declared coolly. 'Ring me when you want to talk business.'

And before Georgia could regain enough composure even to think of a retort, let alone utter it, he had turned on his heel and strode away, disappearing from sight within seconds as he was swallowed up by the crowd.

CHAPTER TWO

FOR perhaps the twentieth time that day, Georgia reached into her handbag and pulled out the small slip of white card, frowning darkly as she studied the words printed on it in an elegant script. Not that she had any need to read them through again; she already knew them, and the telephone numbers, off by heart.

'Ring me when you want to talk business.'

Lucas Mallory's drawling voice echoed inside her head, the calculated note of contemptuous dismissal searing over tightly stretched nerves.

'If I did want anything more personal…you would be the last woman on earth I would choose.'

'Damn you!' Georgia muttered aloud, addressing the words to the piece of card as if it was the man himself. 'Damn, damn, damn you! The feeling's totally mutual, and if I never see you again it will be far too soon!'

Given the choice, she would leave the whole thing well alone, tear the card into tiny pieces and deposit it and her unpleasant memories of the meeting with Lucas in the wastepaper bin once and for all.

But she didn't have the choice, that was the real problem. Only that morning her mother had been on the phone, full of gossip and excitement.

'I've booked Wyndhams to do the catering. They did Polly and Tim's anniversary do and it was wonderful. Oh, and we're having that trio that played at Meg's wedding. We'll open the doors between the sitting room and

the dining room so there'll be plenty of room for danc-
ing, and have the buffet in the garden room—with champagne, of course!'

'Of course,' Georgia echoed wanly, but Anna Harding
didn't seem to need any response, being well launched
onto her current favourite subject.

'I did wonder just who I could get to propose the toast,
but when Meg suggested Bryn Walker he seemed the
obvious choice, and he was delighted to be asked.'

'Bryn Walker?' Georgia didn't recognise the name.

'The new manager of the Leeds store, darling! He and
his wife will be coming, of course.'

'But I would have thought that someone closer...'
Never a daughter, of course. 'Perhaps one of his friends.'

'Oh, but then I wouldn't have known just *who* to
choose, and I didn't want to put anyone's nose out of
joint. And, of course, it is such an important anniversary
for Harding's, as well as Dad's birthday.'

And Georgia knew only too well which of those two
events her father would regard as being the most signif-
icant. His membership of the Harding dynasty meant
much more to him than his position in his own family.

'Of course,' she said again, and this time her mother
caught the strained note in her voice.

'You *are* coming, aren't you, George?' Her own tone
had sharpened, as if she suspected a possible flaw in her
carefully laid plans.

'Yes, I'm coming,' Georgia hastened to reassure her.
'I wouldn't miss it for the world.'

She hoped she sounded convincing. There was nothing her mother liked less than the suspicion that all was
not right in her rather restricted world. But certainly
Anna's concern seemed to have eased.

'And you're bringing someone?'

With her own feelings still see-sawing up and down
on that particular topic, Georgia could only manage an

inarticulate murmur that might have been agreement in reply.

'Someone special?'

'Could be—'

It was an effort to keep her voice light. Her parents—her mother in particular—would definitely regard Lucas Mallory as 'someone special'. The problem was, could she bring herself to ask him to act as her escort now? And even if she did, would he even consider going to the party with her?

The plan that had appeared so attractive and simple at the outset now seemed to be as fraught with difficulties as a trip to the moon, and on the attraction scale it ranked somewhere well below a mouldy apple riddled with maggots.

'Anyway, we'll meet him next week, won't we, darling?'

Next week. Georgia dragged herself back to the present with a swift mental shake. The party was barely ten days away. So if she wanted Lucas to act as her escort—and after all that was why she'd laid out so much money at the auction—she had better stop vacillating and make up her mind pronto.

If. But did she have any alternative? There wasn't exactly a long queue of handsome, wealthy, successful men lining up at her door, all panting for the honour of escorting her to her father's damned birthday party!

There was only one thing for it, she told herself, and, not pausing long enough to allow for the possibility of second thoughts, she moved purposefully towards the phone, pressing the numbers that were etched into her memory with stiff, jerky movements that echoed the state of her feelings.

'Mallory.'

'Oh—'

If she acknowledged the truth, she hadn't expected

any answer, at least, not from the man himself. She had deliberately chosen his work number, reasoning that at this time of the evening he was unlikely actually to be in his office so that she could leave a message on the answering machine, or possibly with a late-working secretary, either of which she would have found much easier than having to respond to that clipped, curt greeting.

'Hello?'

His voice, not warm at the start, had taken on a distinctly icy edge, one that was too uncomfortably reminiscent of his last words to her for comfort.

'Look, is this some sort of nuisance—?'

'No!'

At last the paralysis that had held her tongue frozen seemed to ease, so that she was able to break in on him hastily. She couldn't bear to think that he might slam the phone down on her, cutting her off so that it would all have to be done again.

'I was expecting a receptionist or...'

'Everyone's gone home but me. I'm not such a slave-driver that I keep my staff working at this time of night, even if *I* have to. But if you don't want to speak to me—'

'No, wait—please, Mr Mallory!'

The silence that greeted her stumbling words was distinctly unnerving. For a long, fraught moment she had the uneasy feeling that, knowing who she was, he might still cut her off, but then, unexpectedly, he laughed.

'My dear Georgia—'

If his silence had been disconcerting, then his laughter and the mocking note in his voice when he finally spoke did nothing to restore any sort of sense of balance. It certainly went no way towards making her feel that his attitude towards her had mellowed in any way since the night of the auction.

'You remember me.'

And he recalled her clearly enough to recognise her voice on just those few words. Georgia couldn't begin to decide how that made her feel.

'Of course I do,' that attractive voice murmured silkily in her ear. 'How could I ever forget my beautiful mistress, particularly when our previous meeting was—'

'Mistress!' Georgia exploded, belatedly realising just what he had said. 'I am no such thing!'

'No?' The smooth voice was filled with a carefully assumed tone of innocence—hurt innocence at that! 'What else would you call someone who owns me outright, so that I am nothing but her slave, bought and paid for...?'

Dear God, she could only pray that he was alone in his office. Her cheeks flamed at simply imagining what anyone else might think at overhearing his side of the conversation.

'Oh, you mean the auction!'

Georgia couldn't decide which feeling was uppermost in her mind, the rush of relief at realising just what Lucas meant, or the shockingly sensual reaction that had run along her nerves like an electric current, tightening her scalp and making all the tiny hairs at the nape of her neck lift in instinctive response.

'I mean that I am yours, body and soul, completely in your power...'

'Will you please stop this?'

Georgia prayed that she didn't sound quite as desperate as she felt. This was like some sort of obscene phone call, except that the sensations his words aroused in her were definitely not the fear and disgust she would have felt if that were the case.

'You were the one who asked me to ring you if I wanted to talk business.'

'Oh, business—'

It was as if she had flung a bucket of icy water in his

face, driving all trace of warmth from his voice and leaving it cold and hard.

'Of course, I was forgetting you want to keep things on a strictly formal footing. In that case, just what can I do to help you, Ms Harding?'

Once again Georgia was a prey to conflicting feelings. She was stunned to find herself mourning the loss of the warmly sensual tone, while knowing all the time that it had been just a carefully assumed pretence, with no foundation in fact.

But what really worried her was the fact that the way he spoke should affect her in any way at all. After all, they were complete strangers, destined only to connect with each other very briefly before moving on again on separate paths, like two ships that pass in the night.

Or at least that was how she hoped their relationship would be. Certainly, it was how she would make sure it would be if she had her way!

'I'd like to discuss our—our—'

Furious with her hesitation, she hunted frantically for the right word.

'Date?' Lucas supplied, with what she felt was an unnecessarily exaggerated helpfulness. 'Assignation?'

'Our *arrangement*!' Georgia managed at last.

'Oh, yes, you said you'd let me know precisely what sort of services you require.'

'I hardly think "services" is quite the right term!'

'You mean you want to define my duties,' Lucas amended, with a smooth courteousness that had her gritting her teeth against a furious retort.

'Duties' wasn't much better, but she decided to let it pass this time.

'You said something about a party, I believe. Was that the truth?'

'Of course it was the truth! What the hell else could it be?'

'I've heard better stories.'

'You've heard…!'

The arrogance of the man! Georgia could only be grateful for the fact that he was on the other end of the telephone wires and so couldn't see the way her mouth had actually fallen open on a gasp of sheer disbelief.

'Mr Mallory, are you implying that I was simply making up the story of needing an escort to a party in order to—to—enjoy the pleasure of your company for twenty-four hours?'

She injected every degree of coldness she could muster into her words in order to make her feelings clear, and was almost surprised not to see ice crystals actually form on the receiver as she spoke.

'You'd be surprised what infantile excuses some women come up with,' he returned blithely, apparently totally unfazed by her attempt to freeze him out.

Kelly had been right! Georgia thought furiously. The man flirted with anything in a skirt! He believed every woman to be fair game, needing only a little encouragement in order to fall flat at his feet, even if she was doing her damnedest to make it clear that she wasn't in the least bit interested!

'But someone who looks like you doesn't need to invent any such story. You only had to ask. In fact, you didn't even need to say anything. If you'd just waited a little while, I—'

'*Mr Mallory!*'

Georgia closed her eyes tight, as if by doing so she could block out the unnerving spell that that soft, enticing voice seemed to be weaving around her senses.

'Lucas,' he corrected irrepressibly, but she ignored him and plunged on, drawing on all her self-control to keep her voice steady.

'I have tried to be polite about this, but you appear incapable of taking in what I'm saying. It seems that I have no option but to spell it out in words of one syllable! I do *not*—repeat, *not*—want to spend any time with you. And no matter how hard you may find it to believe that any woman could resist your much-vaunted attractions, let me assure you that here is one woman at least who is totally immune—*impervious*—to your so-called charms! If the nuclear bomb had dropped and you and I were the only people left alive on this earth I would still not want to spend any more than a minute in your company unless I had to. I am not that desperate!'

'Aren't you?'

'I...'

She had opened her mouth to deny the suggestion furiously, to tell him in no uncertain terms just what she thought of him, when realisation had her stopping dead. It seemed that his impertinent question had been repeated inside her own thoughts, echoing it perfectly, right down to the infuriatingly mocking intonation.

'So tell me,' Lucas persisted. 'If you're not that desperate, then why did you attend the auction at all? Why not just ask some friend to act as your escort? Why did you have to pay for someone and not just anyone, but one particular man—*me*?'

'I don't have any friends—male friends, I mean. At least, not the sort of friends I could ask to help me out in this.'

'No one who'll simply be your escort?' Lucas's tone was frankly sceptical. 'Come off it, Georgia! Any fool—'

'Any *fool* won't do!'

Her outburst fell into a silence that sent a frisson of apprehension shivering down her spine, a silence that grew longer and longer as Lucas stubbornly refused to say a word, obviously waiting for her to speak first. It didn't take too long for his deliberate obstinacy to stretch her nerves almost to breaking point.

'Oh, all right! I don't just want an escort.'

Feeling that she had been backed into a corner, mentally at least, Georgia knew that her grip on her self-control had loosened dangerously.

'I want someone whose reputation precedes him as yours inevitably does. Someone who has the sort of immediate impact you have simply by walking into a room.'

'Well, thanks for the compliment. I didn't know you cared,' was the sardonic retort. 'But I still don't see—'

'And I want someone who'll travel with me to Yorkshire to meet my family, but someone who's not involved in any way. Someone who'll do just as I say and no more. I need someone—a man—who'll act his heart out so that he makes it look as if I'm the centre of his universe, the sun in his sky. Someone who can convince everyone at the party that he is hopelessly, head over heels in love with me, just for one day, and then go, walk out of my life without a word, and never come back.'

She paused, expecting some comment, but none came and she had to go on in order to fill the uncomfortable silence.

'I want a total commitment for that twenty-four hours I've paid for, and then nothing—no arguments, no emotional entanglements, just a clean, sharp break. As I said, strictly business. And because it is a business deal I expected to have to pay very well for such a performance.'

This time the silence that fell when she finally finished speaking had a slightly stunned quality about it, one that had her thinking back over precisely what she had just said. She couldn't stop herself from wincing when she became painfully aware of just how much she had let drop.

What had come over her? she asked herself shakenly, thankful that the fiery colour that flooded her face couldn't be seen by the man at the other end of the telephone wires. Or perhaps that was why it had happened. Perhaps it was simply because she couldn't see him, was unable to judge his reaction from his face, that the restraints that normally controlled her tongue had been loosened, resulting in the uninhibited outburst.

But why didn't he say something—*anything*? As the silence drew out, even longer than before, she was finally forced to wonder whether in fact Lucas was still there. But she knew she hadn't heard the receiver being replaced, and it was *silence* she could hear, not the disconnected buzz of the dialling tone.

Just when she thought that her nerves had been reduced to tangled shreds, that she might scream if something didn't happen soon, she heard his drily drawling tones once more.

'That's a pretty tall order, lady. This party must mean a hell of a lot to you.'

'You could say that.'

Georgia's laugh was weak and shaky, and obviously her voice had had no more strength either.

'What did you say? I didn't catch that.'

'I said, *yes*, damn you, it does! But that's my problem. All I need to know from you is whether you're going to help me. Will you do it? Will you abide by our bargain and be my escort, with all that that implies, for just twenty-four hours?'

Unconsciously she crossed her fingers, twisting them tightly in the telephone cord as she held her breath, waiting for his answer.

'I'll have to think about it,' Lucas said at last after another interminable wait. 'Give me ten minutes.'

And this time he did put the phone down on her, cutting her off abruptly and leaving Georgia staring in shock and confusion at the silent receiver in her hand.

CHAPTER THREE

'LUCAS?'

It took a couple of seconds for Georgia to register just what had happened.

'*Lucas!*'

She shook the receiver angrily, almost as if wishing it was the man himself, but of course it remained stubbornly uncommunicative, the only sound that issued from it the monotonous buzz of the dialling tone.

'Oh, damn you! You arrogant pig!'

How dared he? How dared he just cut her off like that?

Then again, he had said to give him ten minutes, so perhaps...

She waited, scrupulous to the very last second, before she dialled the number again, her fingers tapping restlessly on the chair-arm.

'Pick up the phone, you pig! Answer me!'

But the repetitive sound of the phone ringing on and on at the other end of the line continued unbroken until, in a fury, she slammed the receiver back into its rest, cursing Lucas Mallory savagely as she did so.

So now what? Lucas might be perfect for her plan; she had even admitted as much to him just now, blurting it out without considering the possible consequences. But if he was going to use her declaration of how much she needed him as a weapon against her, a way of manipulating the situation from the position of power that she had inadvertently put him in, then was even perfection worth all the hassle that would inevitably result?

But he was *perfect*. And what were her chances of finding someone even remotely like him to act as a replacement at such short notice? After all, she had already told her mother, or at least hinted that she was bringing 'someone special' to the party, and the thought of facing her father alone after all was a prospect she viewed without any pleasure at all.

'Oh, damn you, Mallory!'

Her fingers clenched around Lucas's card, twisting it as viciously as she wished she could Mr Cool's elegant neck. But even as she did so another thought struck home, one that had her smoothing out the piece of pasteboard and reading the numbers from it once more as she pressed the buttons on her phone with urgent haste.

Of course! He'd needed the ten minutes to get home! No matter how much *she* might want to keep things on a strictly business footing, Lucas Mallory, the man whose nickname 'the fastest man on the track' didn't simply refer to his racing career, would never consider any negotiation with a presentable female on those terms. And if she had any doubts, she had only to recall that he had described her as—what was it?

'Oh, damn!'

Just the thought of that provocatively seductive voice murmuring the words 'my beautiful mistress' had distracted her so that she had pressed the wrong sequence of numbers. Drawing a deep, calming breath, she started again, concentrating fiercely this time.

'Be there!' she muttered as the phone began to ring. 'Please be there!'

Tensed up as she was, it took her several unfocused seconds to realise that the sound she could hear in her left ear was not the same as the one that rang unremittingly in the right. When she finally registered that the loudest, most persistent sound was in fact her front doorbell, she got to her feet in a rush.

'I'm coming!' she called, hurrying down the hallway. 'I'm sorry! I— Oh, *hell*!'

As always, the tight-fitting door stuck awkwardly, and she had to struggle hard to open it.

'I'm sorry! I was on the phone, and I— Oh!'

Flustered, out of breath from her battle with the door, decidedly mentally off balance and with her hair falling in tumbled disarray around her flushed cheeks, she was ill-prepared for the sight that met her eyes.

'What are *you* doing here?'

The smile that Lucas Mallory turned on her was wide and bright, perfectly composed and totally disarming.

'Good evening, Georgia. I'm sorry I'm a bit late, but it took rather longer than I'd calculated to get across town.'

'Longer than…?'

'Give me ten minutes'! All the time that she had been trying to get through to him on the phone he had been on his way here!

'Well, can I come in?'

Lucas sounded mildly amused, almost as if he knew just what she had been through in the interval between the moment he had put the phone down and his unexpected appearance. His smile broadened and Georgia had a sudden, unpleasant mental image of just how she must look—red-faced and with her hair all over the place, dressed unflatteringly in an elderly beige sloppy Joe sweater with brown cord leggings. It must be obvious that she had been very much caught on the hop.

'Or do you want me to wait in the car until you're ready?'

'Ready?' This time she didn't care if her confusion showed. 'Ready for what?'

The tiny quirking of one corner of his beautifully shaped mouth betrayed an impulse to respond with some provocative suggestion, but he resisted the temptation admirably, saying instead, 'For dinner. I take it you weren't planning on going to the restaurant dressed like that.'

The look he turned on her clothes was distinctly un-complimentary.

'I wasn't planning on anything!'

With an effort, Georgia restrained herself from banging her hand against the side of her head to clear the confusion. She felt as if she was appearing in some play where the script was constantly being changed without warning.

'And I don't recall you asking me out!'

'I didn't.' The gleam in those dark eyes was totally unrepentant. 'But it seems the obvious answer.'

'Answer to what? Nothing seems in the least bit obvious to me. Oh, look, you'd better come in.'

Perhaps once inside, back in the security of her own familiar surroundings, she might be able to think clearly again. But, unfortunately for her hard-won composure, the first thing that caught Georgia's eye as she led the way into the sitting room was the telephone receiver, still dangling from the edge of the table where she had dropped it in her haste to answer the summons from the doorbell.

The thought of Lucas realising that she had still been trying to get in touch with him, the possible interpretation that he was capable of putting on that fact, sharpened her voice more than she had planned when she turned to him to ask, 'Now, why are you really here?'

'I told you. I want to take you out to dinner.'

'*Why?*'

One dark eyebrow lifted slightly at her tone, and Lucas's mouth twisted cynically.

'Oh, don't worry, darling,' he drawled tauntingly. 'I've no designs on your body, delectable though it may be. Believe me, I prefer my women with a rather more approachable side to their personality.'

She just bet he did! And if that crack about her 'delectable' body was supposed to flatter her into seeing him in a more favourable light then he'd better think again. She had no delusions about her own appearance, and knew she was certainly not the fantasy female type. The dig about personality was likely to be much closer to fact.

'I just thought that if I was to do my job properly, then we ought to get better acquainted,' he went on.

'Is that really necessary?'

'Well, I'm hardly going to convince anyone that I'm hopelessly enamoured of you if I don't know a single thing about your background.'

'Oh, but—'

Just when she had thought she was getting things back under control once more, he knocked her for six all over again. She really should have thought things through more thoroughly.

The truth was that all she had visualised was the look on her father's face when she turned up at his birthday party with *Lucas Mallory* at her side. But now she was forced to face the fact that there was a great deal more involved in all this than she had anticipated, and *involved* was very definitely the word for the position in which she now found herself.

'I can't see you being "hopelessly enamoured" of anyone,' she muttered, knowing deep down that she also couldn't see him really understanding any of her private reasons for doing this in the first place. 'But surely I don't have to tell you things face to face? Couldn't I just put all the facts in a letter?'

'A business memo, perhaps?' Lucas mocked. 'The file on Georgia Harding: name, date of birth, address...'

The final word sparked off a whole new set of questions in Gerogia's mind.

'And that's another thing. How did you know where I lived?'

His shrug dismissed her concern as unimportant.

'Why is that a problem? I know names and addresses and a whole lot more about all my other business associates.'

'Yes, but I'm not just—'

Too late, she saw the trap he had laid gaping widely beneath her feet, and backed off hastily, but not quite swiftly enough. Lucas had seen her reaction, she realised, seen it and noted it with a smile that was frankly predatory, making her heart lurch uncomfortably.

'In my case I think it's more of an invasion of privacy. If I'd wanted you to know, I'd have told you.'

'And the fact that you *didn't* tell me was far more intriguing than any more direct information, as I'm sure you must know.'

That smile had grown, lighting but not warming the darkness of his eyes in a way that made Georgia think shiveringly of a soaring eagle focusing intently on the innocent rabbit or mouse it had marked out as its prey.

'If you're thinking that I did it deliberately in order to "intrigue" you, then I'm afraid I'll have to disillusion you on that score.'

She could see only too well just how it would arouse his interest, of course.

'I mean, I can see that a man like you, who's used to having women if not actually throwing themselves at your feet, then at least coming running if you so much as click your fingers—'

'You have a decidedly exaggerated idea of my appeal, Ms Harding,' Lucas drawled with lazy mockery. 'Or is

it that your opinion of your own sex is so very low that
you believe they have so little respect for themselves as
to behave as you say?'

'You're a fine one to talk about *respect*!' Georgia
flung at him. 'Particularly where women are concerned!'

That barb struck home, the long back stiffening in
response, the dark head coming up, granite eyes blazing
into hers.

'And just what is that supposed to mean?'

Oh, damn, she'd gone a bit too far, said more than
she had meant to.

'I read the papers!'

'And believe every word?' he demanded cynically. 'I
gave you credit for rather more intelligence than that.'

Georgia wasn't at all sure how to respond to the deliberately double-edged compliment, feeling as if she
had been backed into a very uncomfortable corner.

'And I have a friend—'

'Oh, of course! And does this friend have a name?'

Georgia shifted awkwardly from one foot to another,
feeling that she had been pushed into a corner yet again.

'I promised I wouldn't say.'

'I see.'

The two syllables were so brutally clipped and curt
that they made Georgia think uncomfortably of the
sound of a door slamming shut, or the trap that she had
imagined earlier snapping closed with bone-crushing
force.

'So you can throw out accusations, put any slur you
fancy on my reputation, and I'm not even allowed to
know the name of your informant?'

He was dangerously close to losing that famed cool,
Georgia realised nervously, his potentially dangerous
temper only being held in check by ruthless control.

'You probably wouldn't even remember her. And, besides, I don't think your *reputation*—' deliberately she

gave the word a sardonic intonation '—needs any help from me.'

'So that's the way it is, is it? You've barely spoken more than a couple of hundred words to me and yet already you have me tried and convicted, found guilty without even so much as a chance to state my case.'

Georgia had to acknowledge that his assessment of the situation was close to the truth. The admission made her conscience prick her unmercifully, because normally she tried to be scrupulously fair.

'And are you trying to claim that *all* of those newspaper reports were untrue? That you haven't been linked with—oh, let me see…'

She listed names off the top of her head, counting each one off on her fingers as she did so. He let her get to nine before breaking in on her.

'No, I won't. I can't deny that they were once part of my life.'

'With the emphasis on *once* and *part*, I presume.'

Georgia was disturbed by her own reaction. She felt almost raw inside in response to the way he hadn't even tried to reject her accusation of promiscuity, and yet should that bother her? If he wanted to risk his life by being so thoroughly irresponsible, then that was his own stupid business. She had no reason to be disappointed to find he was just as the Press had painted him.

'And are you trying to say that *you* have never split up with a boyfriend, a lover? That *you* never realised that seeing someone was a mistake or that it was time to move on?'

'Of course not!'

'Of course not,' he echoed cynically. 'And I suppose that the so-perfect Ms Harding has never been dumped by someone you thought cared, someone—'

'All right, you've made your point!'

'Aha!' Those dark eyes gleamed with unholy triumph.

The eagle had swooped down on its prey with deadly accuracy. 'Caught you on the raw then, did I?'

Hating him, though whether for his triumph or for seeing through her defences she wasn't sure, Georgia drew a deep breath.

'Oh, yes, all right! I've had my share of broken relationships.'

'So tell me about them.'

Georgia blinked hard in shock, unable to believe her eyes as Lucas shrugged off his elegant pale grey jacket, tugging his tie loose at his throat and unbuttoning his shirt collar before settling himself in a chair. He leaned back comfortably, crossing one leg over the other with every appearance of total ease.

'I beg your pardon?'

'Tell me about them,' he repeated, resting his head on the soft cushions and looking up, straight into her face, clearly noting the hectic colour that flared in her cheeks, the glitter of irritation in her eyes.

'I'll do no such thing! Just what do you think gives you the right to barge in here—?'

'You did,' he inserted into her tirade with infuriating calmness, adding with exaggerated care, 'And I didn't barge, you invited me in.'

'But only because I had no choice! And I *didn't* give you the right to pry into my life.'

Those dark grey eyes widened in an expression of carefully assumed innocence.

'Oh, but you did, Gia. From the moment you lifted your pretty little hand in order to bid at that auction you made me part of your life, and, inevitably, that also meant that you became part of mine. Naturally, I was curious about the woman who thought that twenty-four hours of my company was worth the outrageous amount you ended up paying, donation to charity or not.'

'No.' Her mind flinched away from the idea of being

part of his life. That was not what she wanted at all. 'It's a business deal—no involvement.'

But Lucas ignored her interjection and continued as if she hadn't spoken.

'And, of course, if you want me to act as if I've known you for some time, then the little I already know isn't enough.'

'It's more than—' A thought struck her, a vital question that she had wanted to ask earlier but other things had distracted her. 'How *did* you find out where I lived?'

His smile was slow, lazily taunting.

'I asked questions. You'd be amazed how many people were keen to tell me all about my new "owner".'

'No, I wouldn't,' Georgia growled. She was well aware of the fact that her action in bidding at the auction—for anyone, but especially for Lucas—had caused more than a flutter of interest. It wasn't the sort of behaviour people expected of her.

'So you know about your reputation, do you?'

If that was supposed to throw her, then she was more than happy to spoil his moment of pleasure by pulling that particular rug out from under his elegantly booted feet.

'As the Ice Maiden?' she returned, with a coolness that made it plain where the nickname had come from, matching anything he had ever displayed. She even managed a smile, although it wasn't reflected in her eyes in any way. 'Of course I know.'

'Why do they call you that?' To her surprise, Lucas sounded as if he really wanted to know.

Georgia lifted her shoulders in a shrug that defined the subject as being totally unimportant to her.

'They think that any woman who puts her career first and concentrates on it to the exclusion of anything or anyone else must be very strange or fundamentally frigid.'

'And yet in a man they'd admire it.'

'Precisely.'

She wasn't going to admit that he had surprised her, that his comment was the last thing she had expected. She had anticipated further uncomfortable probing into just why she put her career before relationships.

'But of course you'd understand. After all, that's how you run your life.'

'Used to,' Lucas corrected, continuing without any further elaboration, 'And is this why you need an escort?'

'Mmm.'

Georgia couldn't quite meet those probing eyes, feeling irrationally that if she looked into them he might actually be able to see right into her thoughts and realise that the party was only part of her problem, that there was a great deal she was leaving unsaid.

'I really think you should have dinner with me.'

'And *I* really think that there's no need for that. I can tell you all you need to know without any fuss.'

'No, you can't.'

'Of course I can!'

Lucas shook his head adamantly, lounging back in his chair once more, his comfortably relaxed posture and the smug smile playing around the corners of his mouth infuriating her further.

'Would you mind telling me just what is going to be so damn difficult about it? I really can't see any problem at all. After all, you seem to have already started the process on your own. I mean, how *did* you find out where I live?'

'As I said, I asked questions.'

'You asked questions,' Georgia said hollowly, not liking the idea at all.

'And I got some very interesting answers.'

That caught her attention, though she couldn't have

said whether she was intrigued or angry at the thought of him prying into her private life.

'Such as?' She couldn't help herself.

'Oh...'

Lucas assumed a thoughtful expression, as if considering his options.

'Such as the fact that you're twenty-seven, unmarried, with no steady man in your life at the moment. You have your own interior design company and I gather you're building up quite a reputation.'

'That's not interesting!' Georgia scoffed. 'It's common knowledge.'

'It's interesting to *me*.'

'You can't expect me to believe that! After all, you're the one with the high profile lifestyle, the international reputation, why should you take any int—?'

'And why not?'

Lucas startled her by getting to his feet as he spoke, coming towards her soft-footed as a cat, his eyes so deep and dark they seemed to hold hers with mesmeric force.

'Why not?' he murmured in a very different voice, one that seemed to wind itself around her like warm smoke, weaving through the rich strands of her hair, feathering over her skin, raising tiny prickles of awareness all over her body. 'Why shouldn't I be interested in—fascinated by—the most beautiful woman in the room at that charity auction? A woman whose clear, bright eyes make me think of a young doe in a forest glade, whose skin is as soft and delicate as the ripest peach...'

Reaching out with slow grace, he took her hand very gently, and entranced, hypnotised by his eyes and his voice, she couldn't resist him, couldn't fight against the seductive spell he was weaving. She almost believed he had the power to charm her soul out of her body like some long ago druid or shamen.

'A woman whose hair gleams the colour of a newly opened horse chestnut, whose body could be the model for Botticelli's *Venus*...'

Georgia hadn't even noticed that he had raised her hand, lifting it the final couple of inches to meet his lips. It was only when she felt the warm, soft pressure of his mouth against her fingers that reality broke through the golden trance in which she had been imprisoned.

The burning crackle of response that flared through her nerves from that one point of contact, blazing up her arm and radiating throughout her body, made her snatch her hand away sharply. She would have been unable to ascribe the small cry that escaped her either to delight or distress with any degree of confidence.

'Stop it!'

Her voice was high-pitched and shaking, and she cradled the hand he had kissed against her as if it had actually been physically burned.

'I don't want this! I—I—'

She broke off sharply, stunned into silence as Lucas grinned broadly, his eyes lighting with a devilish, totally unrepentant gleam that mocked her response for the overreaction it was.

'Just practising,' he murmured. 'You said you wanted someone who could make people think that you are the centre of their universe, the sun in the sky.'

That grin widened, became positively malevolent.

'And if I can convince you, then I can convince anyone.'

'Con-vince—' The word cracked disastrously in the middle as the reality of just what he was saying hit home to her. 'You—!'

She couldn't say which was worse, the skill with which he had duped her, or the nagging ache around her heart that told her he had only been able to deceive her so easily because some weak, foolish part of her had actually *wanted* to believe his extravagant protestations. No, not wanted, she hastily corrected herself, but she had listened to them with more attention than was wise.

Instead of which, every ounce of common sense, every trace of self-preservation she possessed should have screamed at her to reject Lucas's attentions out of hand. After all, she knew it was the type of thing he must do to almost every girl he met, and as such it was the last thing on earth she wanted. But somehow, even as she formed it in her mind, the stern admonition didn't quite ring true.

'But *your* reaction was a little lacking in enthusiasm,' Lucas persisted, apparently blithely unaware of her withdrawal. 'You'll need to be a lot more relaxed, more responsive, if we're ever to have anyone believing we're a couple.'

The last word caught on some raw spot in Georgia's strangely vulnerable heart, tugging at it sharply so that she had to struggle to ignore it.

'It's only for a few hours! Just for the party!'

'A few hours can seem a very long time in the wrong company. And I presume that if this party means travelling to Yorkshire, then it also involves the necessity for an overnight stay. Unless, of course, you plan on doing a Cinderella act and disappearing as soon as the celebrations are over. If we're going to keep up this farce for a day or so, and put on a performance that appears even halfway credible, then we'll have to look as if we're comfortable in each other's company, as if we've been together for some time.'

Once again Georgia's heart gave that uncomfortable little kick, making her draw in her breath on a sharp, uneven gasp.

'We have to work on this face to face. So come on, Gia...'

His voice had softened again, becoming huskily cajoling.

'What harm could dinner do?'

Shockingly, disturbingly, it seemed that gentleness
could break through her defences more swiftly and easily
than any more forceful approach. Georgia found herself
considering both his question and the invitation behind
it with unexpected seriousness.

'I—'

But somehow the act of opening her mouth, of forming the single syllable managed to shake her out of the
sense of weakness to which she had almost succumbed.
Not for nothing had Lucas reminded her of her father,
she reflected bitterly. Like her parent in her childhood,
and others since, he wanted it all his own way, and to
hell with anyone else.

She wasn't going to be bulldozed into doing as he
wanted! She wouldn't let him take charge in this way,
wouldn't surrender control to him. If she did then he
would take over completely, make her play by his rules,
and that was not how she wanted things to be at all.

'No,' she said firmly, feeling as if she had just taken
a hasty step backwards from a carefully baited trap over
which her unwary foot had been hovering. 'I told you,
I want no personal involvement in any of this. It's
strictly business, and nothing more.'

Her sharp tone had Lucas's grey eyes narrowing dangerously, the muscles in the forceful jaw drawing tight
around his mouth and thinning it to a hard, slashing line.

'Strictly business,' he snapped. 'Fine. But even in my
business deals I try to give the best I can, and to do that
I'll need to know all the facts. If you can't—'

Abruptly he broke off, shaking his dark head before
swinging away from her, looking round for his discarded
jacket.

'No, this isn't going to work,' he told her, snatching

the expensive garment up from the chair on which it lay and pulling it on, the controlled force of his movements betraying his mood and the difficulty he was having in keeping his anger at her prevarication in check. 'It's been a mistake from the start, so let's just call the whole thing off before we make matters worse. We'll say goodbye now and put it down to experience.'

Georgia couldn't believe what she was hearing.

'But I—'

'Oh, yes, the money—the donation you made in order to secure my services,' Lucas interrupted cynically. 'Well, don't worry. I'll pay it all back, every last penny. There'll be a cheque in the post tomorrow.'

'It doesn't matter!' He had completely misinterpreted her reaction. That hadn't been what was in her mind at all.

'Oh, yes, it does,' he countered coldly. 'I never enter into any agreement where I can't deliver the goods exactly as ordered.'

His mouth twisted into a grim travesty of a smile as he held out a hand.

'Goodbye, Ms Harding. I wish I could say it's been nice knowing you.'

Georgia tried to force herself to say something, anything, but her tongue seemed to have stuck to the roof of her mouth, leaving her as incapable of speech as she was of action. She saw his face harden even further, the proffered hand falling to his side as he turned towards the door.

It would be so much easier to let him go, she thought drearily. Right now all that planning, the scheme that she had thought so clever, so uninvolved, so *businesslike* was unravelling right before her eyes. In fact, she couldn't even begin to imagine why she had thought of it in the first place.

No, she corrected herself, there was nothing wrong

with the scheme. It was just that Lucas Mallory hadn't turned out at all as she had expected. She had picked the wrong man, that was all.

But he was the only man available, cold realism pointed out, bringing her up sharply. How could she hope to find anyone else, anyone she could persuade to go with her, at such short notice? After all, auctions like the one at which she had 'bought' Lucas weren't held every day.

And didn't the fact that he had shown himself to be even more like her father than she had ever dreamed prove, if she had needed proof, that Lucas was just the sort of man she wanted? If she didn't have him at her side for this party, she didn't want anyone.

'Wait!'

Her cry stilled his steps halfway towards the door, and he simply turned his head, staying exactly where he was.

'Perhaps you're right. I mean, I see your point. We *should* talk. I should have realised that you can't just do this cold, so to speak. And—'

The words were strangely difficult to say, seeming to thicken and clog up her throat so that she couldn't get them out.

'And—?' Lucas prompted coldly when she paused to swallow nervously.

'And so perhaps we'd better have this dinner you're so insistent on.'

If he'd smiled, if even a hint of triumph or satisfaction had shown in his face, then she'd have retracted at once and pushed him out of the door without so much as a second thought. But Lucas's face remained as impassive as before.

'If that's what you want.'

He started to turn back towards her, but that wasn't what Georgia had in mind. She might have had to give in to him on this, but she was determined to show it was only a minor concession, and one made strictly on her own terms.

'Not tonight. I've had a long day and I'm tired. What about the day after tomorrow, Thursday?'

For an uncomfortably drawn-out moment Lucas seemed to consider, then he nodded slowly.

'Thursday,' he agreed coolly. 'Fine. I'll pick you up around eight.'

It was only when the door had swung to behind him that Georgia admitted to the uneasy suspicion that he had known exactly what had been going through her mind all along; known it and simply waited for her to act as he had anticipated. She had the nasty feeling that she hadn't avoided the trap he had laid at all, but instead had plunged head-first straight into its jaws.

CHAPTER FOUR

'Oh, why did I ever let myself get talked into this?'

Georgia addressed the words to her reflection as she surveyed herself in the mirror, unable to avoid meeting her own eyes and so seeing the way that an attack of nerves had changed their clear hazel into something approaching a dark mossy green. The deeper colour seemed to be emphasised by the tawny eyeshadow and ebony mascara she had used, so that they looked like shadowy woodland pools against her creamy skin.

Why hadn't she refused to go along with the idea of dinner all together? And yet Lucas was right. If she was strictly honest with herself, she knew, deep down, that that was the case—they did need to spend some time together.

But it didn't help when just to think of him, just the sound of his name inside her head, made her prickle all over in a reaction that was either nervous or irritable. For the life of her, she couldn't decide which—probably both. It was going to take every single second of this dinner tonight to get her even to come close to relaxing in his company, let alone bring herself to the point of being able to pretend that the two of them were—

'A couple...'

It sounded even more disturbing spoken aloud like that, even worse than when Lucas himself had used those same words a few days before. Now they seemed to come with overtones of feeling, of commitment.

But, no, she was simply being silly—downright ridiculous, in fact! She wanted no such thing, and neither, by his own declaration, did Lucas. Somewhere along the line her thoughts had gone way off track, and now was the time to get them right back on it again. This *association* between Lucas Mallory and herself was as it had always been: strictly business, nothing more, and she would be every sort of a fool if she let any fanciful imaginings intrude into it.

Her thoughts were interrupted by the sound of the doorbell, sending her eyes once more to the mirror to check on her appearance.

The cool ivory trouser suit with its long jacket and matching waistcoat-style top underneath was elegant without being over dressy, its pale colour a perfect foil for the copper-coloured hair fastened in a smooth braid at the back of her head. With the subtle use of make-up to flatter her rather strong features, she looked exactly as she wanted to appear: a confident, assured business-woman about to conduct a meeting with a prospective client.

'Strictly business,' she told herself as she walked downstairs. After all, she knew that routine like the back of her hand.

Switching on a controlled smile, she opened the door, turning smoothly to the man on the threshold.

'You're very prompt.'

Her composure almost deserted her in the moment that her eyes met those dark grey ones head-on, the impact seeming to strike sparks in the air. Suddenly she felt disturbingly as if she had been caught in the cascade of burning brilliance that had exploded from some glorious firework, so that she drew in her breath sharply, hunting for control.

'Punctuality is an essential part of courtesy,' Lucas returned. 'And courtesy has closed many a business deal when the hard sell hasn't worked.'

'And you've decided against the hard sell with me?'

She had forgotten how deep his eyes were, how dark and devastating in his strong-boned face under the blue-black hair, and she genuinely didn't remember his being quite so tall and imposing.

His lean frame was perfectly enhanced by the superb cut of his silvery grey suit, emphasising the impressive width of those straight shoulders in contrast with the narrow waist and hips. The supple fabric clung to long, muscular legs in a way that dried her throat disturbingly, and her feeling of disorientation was aggravated by the blinding smile he directed straight into her face.

'I thought I was the one who had to be sold on this idea,' he pointed out, the dry irony with which he laced the words catching on something unexpectedly raw in her mind.

'Well, if you don't want—' she began, only to break off abruptly when he held up a hand to silence her.

'Gia, don't. Don't start that all over again. I thought we agreed that we would be partners on this. That *is* why I'm here tonight.'

Partners. It sounded safely uninvolved, reassuringly so.

'You're right.' Determinedly she swallowed down that disturbingly unsettled feeling. 'I'm ready; I'll just get my bag.'

He had the car door open for her by the time she returned, and she slid into the front seat with a gracious smile that owed much to the couple of moments' careful deep breathing that she had used to collect herself while inside the house.

'This isn't one of your classic cars,' she commented, well aware of the fact that the sleek vehicle's smooth lines, although obviously extremely expensive, were very modern indeed.

'No, it's not,' Lucas confirmed, turning the key in the ignition. 'I don't use them for entertaining.'

'Not even to impress a client? I would have thought

that a touch of elegance would have a most favourable effect.'

'My clients are usually much more impressed if they get to drive a car themselves. Is that why you're disappointed?'

'Not at all.' Georgia covered up hastily. 'But I think my father would be if you turned up in something like this.'

'So it was my occupation that led you to choose me rather than any other considerations when you put in that outrageous bid? It was simply the car's bodywork you wanted to get your hands on.'

'It certainly wasn't anything else!' Georgia retorted, refusing to rise to the bait of his mock-despondent tone and the carefully assumed look of disappointment in those granite eyes, and steadfastly ignoring his outrageous emphasis on that word 'bodywork'. 'Any more than you would have chosen *me* for this dinner voluntarily.'

'Well, we'll just have to agree to differ on that topic,' Lucas returned obscurely. 'Interesting though it would be to pursue it.'

'Where are we going?' Deliberately Georgia refused to follow him down the provocative path his thoughts seemed to be taking.

'I've no idea,' was the unexpected return. 'I thought that was up to you.'

The swift, sidelong glance he shot at her stunned face was touched with a gleam of amusement, one that grew swiftly as full realisation dawned on her.

'You did say this was strictly business, and as I am the one being employed by you—'

'But I thought—'

She knew from the way his wide mouth quirked up at the corner that he was only too well aware of just what she'd thought, and that he'd anticipated it all along.

'That I would pick our destination and book a table?

Oh, no, my lovely, that only happens on a *date*, which of course this is not, and not always then in these enlightened days.'

'But you were the one who suggested dinner!'

'And you were the one who hedged the invitation round with all those conditions,' he tossed back at her. 'So, seeing as you were so insistent that this was all business and strictly no pleasure, I thought I'd leave all the arrangements in your so-capable hands.'

Georgia knew that her cheeks were flaming with embarrassed colour, her composure badly shaken by the ease with which he had wrong-footed her so completely.

'But I haven't— I never thought—'

'I didn't think you would have,' Lucas returned complacently. 'Which means it's just as well I ignored you and went ahead and booked a table at Voltaire's just in case.'

'*You*—!'

A volatile mixture of fury and the urgent desire to have the ground open up and swallow her deprived Georgia of the ability to think of any insult bad enough to throw at him. Her mood was in no way improved by the unrepentant grin he turned on her briefly before turning his attention back to the road.

'You set me up for that, didn't you?' she demanded furiously.

'Just wanted to be sure,' was the nonchalant reply.

'Sure of what?'

'Exactly how you wanted to play this.'

'You *know* how I want to—how I want things to be.'

The look he gave her this time was frankly sceptical.

'And if you can't accept that, we'll just turn right round and go back.'

Her determination to sound firmly in control was threatened by her voice's unfortunate quaver on the last word as the thought struck her that if Lucas refused to co-operate she wasn't at all sure of her ability to make him do as she asked.

'Oh, I can accept it.' The mockery in the drawling tone set her nerves on edge. 'The problem is, can you?'

Georgia's teeth snapped together with an audible click as she clenched her jaw against the furious retort that would, she suspected, have him doing just as she had said—turning the car and heading straight back to her house. It was what she had declared she wanted, but really it couldn't be further from the truth. It would mean abandoning her plan before it even had time to start.

'If for some reason you are still suffering from the delusion that my choice of you at the auction had anything personal in it, then let me disabuse you of that fact,' she declared, with such freezing hauteur that she fully expected the words to form in drops of ice on the windscreen in front of her.

'I know. It was my *car's* controls you wanted to play with,' Lucas murmured sardonically.

'I've told you, it certainly wasn't *yours*!' Georgia flared, only to find that a sudden memory of a quotation about a lady protesting too much in order to hide her true feelings had her wishing her words back. She regretted them all the more when she saw how Lucas's smile grew, leaving her with the disturbing idea that those very same words were in his thoughts too.

'Well, we'll have to agree to differ on that subject as well. And as to turning and going back, it seems a dreadful waste of time seeing as we're almost at the restaurant now, and I happen to be extremely hungry. So why don't you just go along with the original idea?'

'Do I have any choice in the matter?' Georgia growled, and was rewarded by the sort of dazzling smile that she felt sure must have knocked other women completely off balance in the past. Certainly, even prickling all over as she was, it had the most disturbing effect on her, as she was sure it was meant to.

'Of course you do,' Lucas murmured blithely, manoeuvring the powerful car into a parking space. 'You can go back to your empty house and heat up a TV dinner from the freezer, or you can enjoy a delicious meal here in pleasant surroundings and conduct this business deal in a perfectly civilised manner.'

Put like that, she would have been a fool and an ungracious one at that if she'd disagreed. But all the same Georgia was uncomfortably aware of the way that she had been gently but firmly edged into a corner, with her back very much up against the wall.

'If it will make you feel any better, I'll let you pay for the food,' Lucas told her, with the air of someone making a major concession in the cause of peace, adding cajolingly, 'I managed to get the last table they had free tonight.'

'Oh, all right then! But it wouldn't have been a TV dinner!' she added, determined to salvage something of her pride. 'I'll have you know that I'm considered rather a good cook.'

'I never doubted it for a moment,' he assured her. 'But the chef here has a string of awards to his name, so we might as well see if he deserves them, don't you think?'

'You're probably right,' Georgia conceded, privately acknowledging the uncomfortable probability that once again she had been trapped into doing precisely as he had planned all along.

As they made their way into the elegant restaurant her mental discomposure was worsened by her intense physical awareness of the man at her side. His closeness affected her in a way that made all the tiny hairs on the back of her neck lift in some instinctive primitive response that made it difficult to think, forcing her to concentrate hard to simply put one foot in front of another without tripping.

Lucas's hand at her elbow was simply a gesture, an automatic courtesy, but all the same the warmth of his palm burned through the fine crêpe of her jacket, the musky scent of his aftershave tantalising her nostrils as she hastily suppressed a shiver of reaction before it gave her away to him.

Somehow she made it through the routine of scanning the menu and ordering a meal, though she forgot what she had chosen almost as soon as she had asked for it. She knew she wouldn't have much appetite when it came anyway.

When the wine was poured she reached for her glass with a sense of something close to desperation, hoping that the cool tartness of the pale liquid would ease the unsettled sensation that had affected every cell in her body. She needed something to ease the way her blood was heating steadily, threatening to melt her veins and making her head pound in discomfort.

'Don't look so petrified, Gia.' Lucas's voice was low and husky. 'I'm not going to pounce on you. I promise I won't do anything you don't want me to, so just relax.'

'I *am* relaxed! It's just— What did you call me?'

He had used that name in the car too, she recalled, when she had been too strung up to comment on it, and again on that first night at her house.

Lucas's response to her question was an enigmatic smile as he toyed with his wine glass. He twisted the fine crystal round and round so that the pale wine caught the glow of the candle, making it splinter into a thousand tiny fragments, reflected over and over like the patterns in a kaleidoscope.

'I'll tell you if you answer a question for me too. That seems fair, doesn't it? You ask, then I do. Turn and turn about.'

'Fair enough.'

Once again Georgia felt that she had been left with no choice. If she didn't agree, he would simply refuse to answer any of her questions, leaving her checkmated as before. But at last she thought she was beginning to get something of the measure of this man. She had been right when she'd thought that he reminded her of her father. The two men were very much the same in that they didn't like to take second place in anything.

For his own private reasons, Lucas might have agreed to take part in the charity auction, but perhaps he hadn't quite thought about every aspect of it. He didn't seem to have calculated how much it would grate on him to be forced to play the subsidiary, the slave's role, following instructions rather than giving them.

Even on such a brief acquaintance with him she could see that having to concede to anyone, but particularly to a woman, was anathema to him. That was obviously why he was determined to try and get the upper hand in whatever way he could.

'So what *did* you call me?'

'Gia?' The intonation he gave it implied that she had known very well what he had said. 'Why, don't you like it? I think it suits you.'

'What's to like or dislike?'

She wouldn't admit to the disturbing flutter deep in the pit of her stomach at the sound of his voice. Its sudden softness had turned the unexpected, shortened version of her name with its almost Italian pronunciation into a seductive whisper, close to a caress in itself.

'My name is Georgia. My friends call me Georgie, my family George.'

The twist to his unsmiling mouth told her exactly what he thought of that.

'You don't approve?'

'What's to approve or disapprove?' Deliberately he almost echoed her own words of a moment before. 'What bothers me is just why a supremely female creature like you let herself be lumbered with such a masculine-sounding name.'

Fortunately for Georgia, the waiter chose that moment to arrive with their starters, providing a welcome distraction. The few seconds enabled her to regain some degree of composure and swallow down the mouthful of wine over which her throat had closed so suddenly.

'Is that your question?' she asked when they were alone again, managing not to show how close he had come to catching her on the raw. 'Or were you just thinking aloud, speaking off the top of your head?'

'I never say anything off the top of my head. And, that being so, you can believe me when I say I have to wonder why such a simple question upsets you so much.'

'I'm not upset!'

The look Lucas turned on her, the questioning lift of one dark eyebrow, told her only too clearly that she hadn't convinced him at all. And no wonder, she told herself, when her voice came and went in such a disturbing way, sounding like a very old, worn and scratched seventy-eight. She prayed that the flickering candlelight concealed the betraying sheen in her eyes that made them overbright in a way that contradicted her declaration eloquently.

'At least, not by anything *you've* said.'

'Which begs the interpretation that someone else did the upsetting.'

The guess was far too perceptive, too close for comfort, and suddenly she could no longer meet those eyes, deep and intent in the candlelight. He leaned towards her, one strong hand covering her own where it rested on the immaculate white tablecloth.

'Who was it, Gia?' The attacking quality had gone from his voice so that it sounded soft and enticing, seeming to weave around her delicately like the smoke from the candles curling up towards the ceiling. 'Who hurt you, made you so defensive? Was it some other man?'

Of course, that would be the only explanation he would come up with. Well, he had come close, but not in the way he believed.

'No— I—' How had she given herself away? 'What makes you think you know?'

'I don't know, but I could easily hazard a guess from all you've let drop.'

'But I never said a thing.'

'Not deliberately, perhaps, but there were plenty of clues for anyone who cared to look: your concern about this party, for one. And it's for your father? His birthday?'

Silently Georgia nodded. 'His sixtieth.'

'And that's so very important to you?'

'Isn't everyone's father's birthday important?'

It was a vain attempt to regain lost ground, and she knew she hadn't succeeded when she saw his smile.

'Important, yes, but not so dramatically so as to make someone act completely out of character.'

'Out of— I don't know what you mean!'

'Well, I'll tell you, shall I?'

Effortlessly he held her gaze, the food, their surroundings, the buzz of conversation from everyone else in the restaurant all totally forgotten as he listed each fact with the coldly logical rationale of a lawyer in a court-case. The problem was that Georgia was incapable of deciding whether he was counsel for the prosecution or the defence.

'From the start it was plain that you weren't comfortable with the auction. Everyone else treated it as a joke, a laugh, but you were deadly serious. Anyone watching the audience would have known that your decision to bid wasn't at all what they expected from you.'

Georgia bit down hard on her lower lip in order to hold back the response that had almost escaped her. There it was again, that worrying implication that he had seen her long before she had been aware of him. It seemed that he had been watching her at least from the moment she had raised her hand to bid, and perhaps well before. The thought sent shivers of apprehension down her spine.

'You obviously wanted *me* and me alone. Why else would you put in such an inordinately large bid—one that no one else was likely to top, even for charity, unless they were out of their minds or, like you, desperate?'

'I was *not*—'

Too late, she realised how the vehemence of her protest betrayed her, revealing too much of her inner turmoil. Hastily she tried to bite it back, but not before Lucas had caught the raw note in her voice, and with a sardonic lift of one eyebrow he questioned the truth of her declaration.

'Let's just say you had more invested in this than the simple night out or blind date that the auction's organisers had planned,' he murmured, in the sort of voice that made her think of a trained horseman speaking to a highly-strung thoroughbred, calming it softly when nerves threatened to get out of control. 'If that was all that had been involved, then I'd have thought you'd had some sort of knock-back, a blow to your self-esteem—that perhaps you were trying to show someone who'd—'

'You think I'd indulge in vulgar displays like that in order to bolster my *self-esteem*? That you are such a catch—'

Lucas shook his dark head, his eyes never leaving hers.

'As I said, *if* that was all then I'd have thought that. I'll admit it was what went through my mind at first, but then, when I tried to introduce myself, you were so—' he chose his words with care '—so unapproachable as to be downright hostile. It was as if you really didn't want me anywhere in your life and yet you couldn't help yourself; you *had* to do this.'

Georgia couldn't suppress a shudder at the thought of how much he had picked up. She had believed herself to be so in control, and yet this man had seen right through her defences.

'I thought it was me, that there was something you'd heard or believed that you just couldn't stand, and yet at the same time it was obvious that it was me you wanted. You were blowing hot and cold, giving come-hither signals—'

'I most definitely was not!'

'And then freezing me out again.' Lucas ignored her furious interjection. 'In the end the only conclusion I could come to was that whatever this man was, I was too. That was when you told me I reminded you of your father.'

Georgia's teeth dug into her lower lip so hard that she thought she might actually draw blood. She had spoken without thinking but he had homed in on it.

'It was just a casual remark.'

'Perhaps. But then on the phone you made it plain that you didn't just want someone who would *escort* you to the party. You needed someone who would make it look as if you were very special to them, as if you were lovers.'

'No!'

In spite of herself, Georgia couldn't hold back the protest. She didn't know why the word 'lovers' coming from that sensual mouth and spoken in that softly emphatic way should have such an effect on her, only that she couldn't control the immediate and instinctive twisting of her sensitive nerves as she heard it.

'A couple, then.' Lucas shrugged off her response. 'But you didn't say why. Don't you think it's time to stop pussyfooting around and tell me what you really want?'

'I—don't know what you mean.'

Deciding attack was a better form of defence than the one she'd been using, she forced herself to meet that dark gaze head-on.

'Are you trying to claim that really I'm saying I want you as my lover? Because if so—'

'I'm saying I don't know what the hell you *do* want, and I'm not all that sure that you do either. But if you want me to come along with you on this you're going to have to give me a few more facts.'

'Facts,' Georgia echoed, dropping her eyes at last as she toyed with her knife, staring at it fixedly so as not to have to look into that watchful face any longer.

The problem was that it wasn't just the facts that she didn't want to reveal. Deep down inside she was suddenly sharply and worryingly aware that her reluctance was founded on an unwillingness to let *Lucas* know anything more about her than strict politeness demanded.

To give him the intimate, personal facts he demanded seemed to her to smack of putting herself in his hands. It would give him a power over her that would make her feel frighteningly vulnerable, exposed in a way that she had never been in her life before—except once.

'You've got it all out of proportion.' In desperation, she tried one last attempt at bluffing. 'It's not really all that important.'

'You'll have to forgive me if I don't exactly believe you.'

Lucas's wave of his hand dismissed her words with a touch of scorn.

'After all, it's not every day that I find myself being bought by a woman who wants me to—what was it?—convince everyone that I'm hopelessly, head over heels in love with her, just for one day, and then walk out of her life and never come back. Does that sound ''not really all that important'' to you?'

Georgia couldn't find any words to answer him, and she knew that the way she'd flinched at the brusque summary of her demands hadn't escaped those sharp grey eyes. Put like that, it sounded so much more unreasonable than she had ever intended.

'I think you owe me rather more than "I—don't know what you mean."' He mimicked her tone with deadly accuracy, bringing her head up sharply.

'I don't owe you anything, Mr Mallory! I—'

'We agreed on Lucas,' he cut in coldly.

'*We* agreed on nothing! I told you what I wanted, and—'

'And I'm expected just to go along with it, without question or—'

'That's what I paid for!'

'What you *paid* for,' Lucas echoed with a grimace of disgust, as if the words left a sour taste in his mouth. 'So we're back to that again, are we? Look, lady, you may have "bought" me, putting me under a moral obligation to the charity, but that doesn't mean you own me body and soul. I don't go in for deals, business or otherwise, where I don't know the full facts.'

'Exactly what are you trying to say?' Georgia put in, each syllable cold and precise.

'Just this,' Lucas flung back at her, obviously driven close to the edge of what patience he had left. 'Either you tell me the whole truth about this situation or the deal's off. Is that exact enough for you? You tell me just what is behind all this manoeuvring or I walk out now and you can find someone else to be your slave for the day.'

'I don't think you—'

'I don't *think*. I know!'

Lucas's words slashed through her attempt at protest, his tone harsh and obdurate as the lines into which his dark face was set.

'No explanation, no deal. No deal, no escort. It's your choice, Gia!'

CHAPTER FIVE

'WELL, Gia? What's your answer?'

Georgia shivered at the steely note in Lucas's voice. The five minutes' grace the arrival of their main course had given her had not been by any means enough for her to collect her thoughts and arrange them in any sort of coherent order. Consequently she was no nearer finding the response he demanded than she had been when he had snapped out his ultimatum, flinging it at her as if it were a gauntlet in some form of medieval challenge.

'Come on, it's quite simple. After all, if it's "not really all that important—"' sardonically he quoted her own words back at her '—then why don't you just tell me to go to hell and be done with it?'

Why didn't she? There was no easy way to answer that, because the truth was that in spite of all the difficulties that had arisen since she'd thought of it her plan was still important to her.

The other inescapable fact was that it seemed that every move Lucas made simply confirmed how right she had been to choose him. Even his refusal to co-operate, the domineering way he had taken over, wresting the reins firmly from her grasp, were clear evidence of the fact that he was just the sort of man who could stand up to her father. Lucas would never go down under the steamroller approach that normally flattened everyone in Benjamin Harding's path.

Not Lucas Mallory. He would refuse to be squashed. He would stand up to her father, tackle him face to face.

It would be a match of Titans, the irresistible force meeting the immovable object with a vengeance, so that even thinking of it made her shiver in apprehension. But would he ever go through with it? Certainly not without the explanation he had demanded.

'It's decision time, Georgia. I want an answer.'

The hard, purposeful voice made her shiver again, but in a very different way—that use of her full name was positively worrying. Not knowing how or where to begin, she could only shake her head despairingly, recoiling in shock as Lucas crushed his napkin into a tight ball before tossing it onto the table in front of her.

'Fine,' he declared, the single syllable tight and cold.

The hardness of his expression, the controlled violence of the movement as he pushed back his chair made it plain to Georgia that he had interpreted her gesture as one of refusal to speak. The sudden fear that he might do just as he had said and walk away without a backward glance jolted her into action.

'No, wait!'

Fearful that he hadn't heard, she reached out to catch hold of his arm, her fingers closing around his wrist to restrain him.

'Lucas, please stay!'

For several long, dreadful seconds, as he stood staring down at her hand, the thought that he might reject her appeal, shake off her hand and stride from the room, was uppermost in her mind. She wouldn't be able to hold him if that was what he decided, she knew. Her own fingers looked impossibly white and delicate against the powerful bones and muscles of his arm. But then, apparently reconsidering, he gave her a searching, cruelly assessing look before slowly subsiding back into his seat.

'So tell me,' he commanded coldly.

The words wouldn't come.

'I don't know where to begin. I mean, I don't think

you'll understand. I don't see how any man could, especially not you.'

Lucas mouth compressed tightly at her words.

'And why especially not me?'

'Oh, come on! You, the great Lucas Mallory, World Champion I don't know how many times! Top of the tree—a real star—the perfect *Boy's Own* hero. What would you know about failure or being second best?'

'Don't you believe it,' Lucas put in quietly. 'It hasn't all been winner's trophies and champagne.'

'Hasn't it?'

She couldn't hide her surprise. Lucas moved through life with such total self-assurance that she couldn't imagine him ever meeting an obstacle he couldn't surmount, a problem he couldn't deal with.

Lucas shook his dark head firmly.

'I wasn't born with a silver spoon in my mouth, Gia. Any success I've had I've worked for, and sometimes paid for the hard way. The race track isn't a generous mistress. It takes all you can give it in time, emotion, commitment, even friends.'

'Friends?' His voice had sobered noticeably on the word. 'Was someone—?' Suddenly afraid of being tactless, she couldn't bring herself to complete the sentence, but she didn't have to as Lucas nodded, his expression sombre.

'Tony, my best friend, died in a crash. He was one of the best drivers I knew—the safest. I would have sworn he would never have taken a risk. But he made a tiny mistake...'

The hand which lay on the immaculate linen cloth clenched suddenly in a gesture that was far more expressive than words.

'That was it.'

The dark head moved again as if in disbelief, or an attempt to shake off the shadows of memory.

'He didn't even look hurt; not a mark on him. But he died before they got him to hospital.'

The rigid control that held his tone even was almost more than Georgia could bear, and impulsively she leaned forward to rest her hand on top of his clenched fingers.

'I'm sorry.'

For a brief moment those grey eyes looked into hers, and in the depths of their darkness she could see the flickering flames of the candles reflected in miniature, concealing his innermost thoughts from her.

'But we were talking about you.'

The moment had gone, slipping away from her as smoothly as he eased his hand from under hers, and with it the feeling of empathy, of sharing that she had experienced so briefly.

'Tell me about your problem.' Lucas leaned back in his chair and lifted his wine glass. 'You never know, I might be able to help.'

A few minutes before she might have laughed at the thought. She would certainly have rejected the idea out of hand. But now she was no longer so sure.

In the moment that he had told her of his friend's death he had revealed a previously unseen and unguessed at side of his nature. Brief and unemotional as the account had been, it was as if he had opened a door to a different Lucas, one she suspected he didn't show to many people. He had slammed that door closed again almost at once, but somehow Georgia felt that it didn't quite fit as perfectly as before. Now it seemed that there was the tiniest space around the edge, a chink through which a small amount of light could be seen if you looked hard enough.

'Your problem,' Lucas prompted, growing impatient with her hesitation. 'This man.'

'Not just any man—my father.'

Georgia knew a small sense of triumph at seeing his

sudden frown and knowing that this was not what he had expected.

'He comes from a long line of Hardings, dating back to Victorian times, and in many ways his values haven't changed all that much since his great-great—and probably a couple more greats—grandfather's day. He seems to have inherited them along with the company.'

'Harding's Upholstery?'

'That's right—the family firm. It makes furniture.'

Belatedly, his lack of surprise struck home.

'How did you know that already?'

Even as she spoke the answer came to her.

'Oh, I forgot that you "asked questions",' she muttered, echoing Lucas's own words cynically. 'So you know all this.'

'Bits. I was told that you were one of *those* Hardings.'

Georgia nodded. 'You've heard of the company?'

'Who hasn't? The Harding name has been famous for quality furniture for more than a hundred—'

'Exactly. The Harding name. Handed down from father to son without a break—until now.'

'Ah...' It was a thoughtful sound, one that communicated understanding in more ways than one. '"Until now" meaning that there is no son in this generation?'

'Didn't your sources tell you this?' Georgia muttered, hiding her unease behind a show of belligerence.

'It was just a few enquiries, not intensive research,' Lucas returned mildly. 'But no, no one seems to know very much about your family.'

Hardly surprising, Georgia admitted to herself. After all, she kept that part of her life very much to herself.

'Well, you got it in one.' She couldn't erase the bitterness from her voice. 'There's no son—no heir to carry on the Harding name, take charge of the family firm.'

'And your father being the traditionalist that he is—I suppose that's important to him?'

'It's the end of the world! He inherited Harding's from

his father, who inherited it from his, and so on, right back to Josiah Harding who started it all in the first place. It's an unbroken line, a perfect tradition—the name and reputation being passed on, building a history of its own through the years. And now there's no son to inherit—just three daughters.'

'But surely any woman nowadays…?'

'Not in my father's opinion,' Georgia put in flatly. 'I'm afraid he's not so much Old Man as prehistoric when it comes to Women's Lib. It completely passed him by without even touching. A woman's place is in the home, in the kitchen or in bed, looking after her man, and no woman will ever enter the hallowed portals of Harding's Upholstery.'

'Not even his daughters?'

'Definitely not his daughters.'

'Prehistoric is right. But, hang on a minute, you said *three* daughters.'

'You think I'm taking all this rather too personally?' It wasn't the first time the accusation had been directed at her.

'Well, surely your sisters… Are they older or younger?'

'Older. But you see it didn't matter that they were girls. When Liz and Meg were born were born my parents were both still young. My sisters are ten and twelve years older than me, so there was every chance there would be a son in time. In fact, my father was convinced there *had* to be one. He believed in the old wives' tale that after two babies of the same sex the next one was bound to be different. But it took my mother a long time to conceive again, and…'

Her voice trailed off weakly, her gaze fixed on the flame at the top of the candle.

'And you were the next baby.'

'I was the next baby,' Georgia confirmed flatly. 'Ruining my father's dreams of another generation in the

Harding dynasty. They couldn't try again. There were complications when I was born and Mum was told she was definitely not to get pregnant again. I had to be their last child. And while my father could cope with my sisters being female, I was positively the last straw. He just wasn't interested in another girl.'

'So your name—?'

He really was sharp; far too perceptive for comfort. Georgia suddenly felt a sense of amazement that she had ever thought she could get by without telling him anything.

'The son my father anticipated so confidently was to have been called George. Dad didn't even think to change it when I arrived. It was my mother who made it George*ia*, but Dad usually doesn't bother with the feminine ending. It might have helped if I'd been the right sort of daughter.'

'Kitchen and bedroom,' Lucas inserted on a note of dark irony.

'And pretty,' Georgia added. 'Petite and very delicate—which hardly describes me, does it?'

'Don't fish for compliments.'

'I'm not! I'm being realistic. I'm big-boned and not really feminine.'

'Who the hell said that?'

Lucas's face had darkened, and Georgia had a sudden vivid memory of his voice saying, 'a supremely female creature like you'.

'Your father again? The man's a greater fool than I thought. So, don't tell me—your sisters match up to this impossibly restrictive definition of womanhood?'

Georgia nodded slowly, trying to come to terms with the ambiguous feelings sparked off by the memory of his extravagant praise. He had made her feel special, beautiful, almost, but had almost immediately admitted that he had just been playing her along. So now that flippant 'Just practising' burned in her heart like acid.

'They're both much more like my mother: smaller, daintier and much prettier. And they were quite content to play purely decorative roles and make good marriages.'

'By "good marriages" I presume you mean with men who could keep them in the manner to which they'd become accustomed as your father's daughters?'

'That's right.' Her voice was low.

'And let me guess. They redeemed themselves even further by giving birth to at least one grand*son*.'

'You got it. Two, in Lizzy's case.'

'Heirs for the family firm, even if it has to skip a generation.' Lucas's tone was hard. 'I presume he'll insist that they change their name to Harding?'

'Exactly.'

'Now I think I'm beginning to see how I fit into all this.' This time his intonation was impossible to interpret, with an edge to his words that worried her. Had she confided in him in this way, exposing her innermost feelings, to no avail? Would he still refuse to co-operate?

'This is a way of showing your father that you are as good as your sisters? That you are every bit as feminine as them. And for that you need a man on your arm: husband material.'

'No, not that,' Georgia put in hastily, the sharpness of her tone earning her a cold-eyed stare.

'Oh, no.' Lucas's smile was chilling. 'Of course not. I was forgetting that you want me to leave as soon as the party's over.'

'Well, not immediately.' Not being at all sure just why he found that suggestion so offensive, Georgia decided it was safer to stick to the literal meaning of his words, aiming for lightness. 'Naturally I'd expect to provide you with overnight accommodation, with the party being in Yorkshire. And of course I'd pay for your transport there and back home.'

'*Of course.*'

She didn't need telling that her feeble attempt at humour had fallen painfully flat. It was there in the total lack of warmth in his eyes, the way that wide mouth had set into a thin, hard line.

She was playing this all wrong, Georgia realised. She should have known from the start that a man like Lucas wouldn't take at all kindly to the 'slave' aspect of their arrangement—if they still had an arrangement. Something of which she was none too sure.

He obviously expected to take the lead in all his relationships with the opposite sex, as he had done on the race track. Remembering how he had spoken of the 'fun' he had expected as the result of the auction, she realised that he had probably also anticipated a much more light-hearted approach to the whole thing, not the emotional outpouring she had just subjected him to.

'It'll be a wonderful party,' she told him, with what she hoped was convincingly bright insouciance. 'If there's one thing my mother does well, it's entertain. People in the village still talk in awed tones of my sisters' wedding receptions, and from the sound of things she's pulling out all the stops for this one. You see, it's the hundred and fiftieth anniversary of the founding of Harding's too, so there'll be a family do and a works' party and—'

'And nothing will be done by halves?'

'Oh, no. There's the Harding reputation to maintain.'

Something had jarred in Lucas's response. He wasn't really listening, she thought uncertainly. His mind was apparently on something else.

'Does this mean you'll come?' She couldn't hold back the question any longer.

To her consternation Lucas didn't bother to reply, simply countering her question with another.

'Tell me something, if your family is so well established in Yorkshire, what are you doing down here in London?'

'Running my own business.'

It fell as flat as her earlier flippancy, and she knew that he had detected the 'mind your own business' she had really meant but hadn't dared to say.

'But why here? Why London?'

'There isn't much scope for an interior designer in—'

'Oh, don't give me that! You could have had plenty of work, plenty of *scope* up North as well as here. So why—?'

'All right!'

Georgia found she couldn't hold back any longer, couldn't hide her feelings from him however much she might want to. She didn't care if the hurt of years rang in her voice as she flung her reply into his stony face.

'All right, I'll tell you! I left home because I couldn't work anywhere near my father, and if you want to know why that was, then I'll tell you. I knew that he was just waiting for me to fail. I knew he'd be telling his friends, his contacts, that a woman couldn't run a business, that a woman doesn't have the brains for it.'

'I would have thought that you'd proved that particular prejudice totally unfounded. You've been very successful.'

There was no emotion in the words, nothing to soothe the raw feeling his questions had awoken deep inside. But there was nothing to be gained by detailing the hundreds of petty tyrannies over the years. She couldn't bring herself to describe the pointed ways her father had made it plain that as a replacement for the son he had wanted she was definitely not acceptable.

'Not according to my father. To him it's just ''George's little hobby'', an interest to keep me occupied until I get down to the really important things like starting a family.'

'And have you never wanted to marry?'

The question was so unexpected that, caught unawares, for a couple of seconds Georgia couldn't hide the effect it had had on her.

'Oh, I'd love children, but...' Carefully she lifted her voice up a notch or two. 'Never found the right man, really. Oh, I had my chances, but—'

'Never found the right man,' Lucas echoed flatly, a new and disturbing edge to his voice.

'You said it. Well, that's enough about me.'

More than enough! How had she ended up telling him so much, revealing things she usually kept so very close to her chest? Something about the evening, the atmosphere in the restaurant, the subdued lighting, had acted on her senses, drawing the truth from her. Or was it something about Lucas himself?

No, she was being foolishly fanciful. It was much more likely to be the effect of the wine after the tension she had felt earlier. She rarely drank very much, but tonight the cool drink seemed to have slipped down her throat without her noticing it, and had probably been responsible for loosening her tongue.

To her relief, Lucas took up her attempt to change the subject, moving the conversation on to other, less contentious topics. As a result, Georgia found herself relaxing, appreciating and finally, to her own surprise, frankly enjoying his company as he set himself to be the perfect charming dinner companion.

Their talk ranged over holidays, books they had enjoyed and films they had recently seen. She even found herself able to hold an animated discussion with him when he slated one particular historical epic she had loved, arguing her case with a conviction and enthusiasm that matched his and enjoying the exchange of ideas. The debate only ended finally when they realised that neither of them was going to change the other's mind.

'We'll have to agree to differ,' she said, conscious of the way she was echoing his own words of earlier in the evening.

Lucas nodded, draining the last of his coffee.

'We most definitely will, because if we don't they'll be throwing us out in order to lock up. And as I bring many potential customers here, I prefer to keep in with the management.'

'Is it really that late?'

Looking round, Georgia was startled to see how the restaurant had emptied, that they were alone apart from a discreetly hovering waiter.

'I didn't realise!'

'I'll take that as a compliment.' Lucas smiled. 'And let me assure you that the feeling is mutual. I never noticed the last hour slip away.'

When he smiled like that she came perilously close to knowing exactly what Kelly had meant when she'd said that no one ever said no to Lucas Mallory. There was no denying that the man had charm in mega-doses. He really was quite the most devastatingly sexy man she had ever met—all the more so when he set himself to concentrating that potent charm on a one-to-one basis, the impact of which was almost physical.

'Do you sell many of your cars to women?' she asked curiously as they got to their feet.

'Some, but I have to admit that concern for the image a car presents does tend to be more of a male characteristic than female.'

'That includes me, I'm afraid. As long as it gets me from A to B in security and comfort, and can be relied on not to need too much maintenance, with a reasonable fuel consumption, I don't worry too much whether it's a classic of its kind.'

'Strange.' Lucas turned that smile on her again, creating a sensation in her stomach like the one experienced when plunging down a steeply sloping roller-coaster ride. 'I would have thought that a woman like you, someone who is involved with design and colour in her working life, would appreciate the elegance of, say, an Aston Martin.'

'Oh, I *appreciate* it, on a critical level. But to my mind it isn't so important that I'd pay the inflated prices you charge simply in order to drive one.'

'The prices I charge are never inflated beyond what the car is actually worth. Sometimes a hell of a lot of work has to go into restoring one to the sort of standard my customers expect.'

'I'm sure it does. It's just not important to me; though I have to admit to a secret yearning to get behind the wheel of a...'

'Let me guess,' Lucas put in as her smile and the words faded on the recollection of just why she had always dreamed of one particular car. Another attempt to find some point of contact with her father that, like so many others, had failed miserably. 'A Lotus Elan?'

'A real woman's car, is that what you mean?' Memory made her voice sharp. 'Then, no, I hate to disappoint you, but I wasn't thinking of any such thing. What I actually had in mind was a Morgan—particularly the Plus 8.'

If he was surprised then at least he hid it well, she had to admit. But he'd let the charming mask slip for a moment, reminding her once again of the fact that, no matter how he appeared on the surface, underneath he was very much her father's sort of man.

'Well, I have to admit that that wasn't quite what I'd anticipated, but of course I should have expected *that*. After all, you're not exactly a run of the mill sort of woman. And you haven't disappointed me, Gia. You may surprise, and often do, but you could never, ever disappoint.'

Which was just the sort of clever reply she should have been prepared for, Georgia told herself. But all the same she had trouble adjusting to the way he had turned round her attempt to crush him so that it rebounded on her.

Just how did she interpret 'not exactly a run of the mill sort of woman'? From any other man she was not at all sure it would be a compliment. But when Lucas had used the phrase she'd had no idea as to what had been in his mind.

The one thing she had no doubt about was that she was meant to be feeling just this way. He had wanted her to feel uneasy and unsettled. Lucas used words with the skill of a trained fencer, feinting and parrying until she had no idea exactly in which direction he was really aiming.

But she had to remember that a skill was precisely what it was. Lucas had said that he regularly brought customers to this restaurant, and, in spite of his disclaimer, very probably some of them were women. He must put his consummate social skills to good use on those occasions too, and probably ended up with other conquests as well as a sale.

The charm was not for *her* personally, she told herself reprovingly. With Kelly's experience as a warning example to her, she had no intention of ending up as one of 'Mallory's Moppets'—an all too brief 'pit stop' before he moved on to pastures new. Lucas Mallory went through women as swiftly as he drove his racing cars, or at least he had done when he had been racing competitively. She had to admit that lately there had been far fewer reports in the papers.

'Ready to go?'

Coming out of her thoughts with a jolt, Georgia realised belatedly that while she had been absorbed Lucas had signed the bill without her even being aware of it.

'But I was supposed to pay that!' she protested as they made their way to the car park, not liking the way he had taken matters out of her hands. 'After all, it was my—'

'But I invited you,' Lucas put in smoothly, making her recall the way he had reacted against any suggestion that he was obliged to do as she asked because of the auction. 'You can make me coffee if you like. That'll even things up.'

'Hardly! I know the price of a meal at Voltaire's as well as you, and a measly cup of coffee comes—'

'It will be fine, Gia,' he told her, emphasising his words with a slam of the car door. 'And it will give us an excuse not to end the evening too soon. After all, the night is still young—well, youngish.'

Which left her hard up against the fact that once more she had been outmanoeuvred. 'You can make me coffee,' he had said, not '*Would* you make me coffee?' or even a hint that 'Coffee would be nice.' His directive had been so arrogant that there was no doubt it was a command to be obeyed. He had very much taken over the reins again—if, in fact, she had ever had them in her hands all evening. Suddenly Kelly's comment that no one ever said no to Lucas Mallory sounded in her head again, with a more ominous emphasis.

There was one way to put a stop to this, Georgia resolved as the car drew up outside her home. With her house keys in her hand, she drew a deep breath and sat up straight in her seat. As she turned towards Lucas she could only pray that her face looked more controlled than she actually felt.

'Before we go any further,' she began as coolly as she could manage, 'there's one thing I want to know.'

He almost concealed the faint smile that crossed his face. Almost, but not quite. Georgia's hands clenched on her keys, her jaw tightening as she realised the interpretation he had put on that ambiguous 'go any further'.

'And that is?'

'The reason we're here tonight; the reason we're together at all. I need to know once and for all, are you going to help me with this party or not?'

For a long, deliberately drawn out moment he appeared to consider, his face unreadable in the shadowed car, eyes hooded, hiding his thoughts from her. Then, just as her patience had stretched unbearably thin and was in danger of snapping altogether, he reached forward, pulling the key out of the ignition and tossing it carelessly in the air, catching it one-handed as it descended.

'We'll discuss that over coffee,' he said, and with light fingers eased her own keys from her stunned grasp and was out of the car before she could protest, leaving her with no option but to follow him.

CHAPTER SIX

'YOUR coffee!'

Georgia set the cup down on the table with a distinct crash, not caring that her action betrayed the disturbed state of her innermost feelings. She didn't want to make him coffee, didn't want him in her house to discuss anything, or for any reason whatsoever.

What she wanted was for Lucas to agree to escort her to the party, arrange a time to pick her up on the day, and then go.

'Something wrong?' the subject of her furious thoughts enquired, his carefully solicitous tone setting her teeth on edge.

Correction, she told herself. What she wanted was simply for Lucas to leave as soon as possible, and she really didn't give a hoot one way or another whether he agreed to anything about the wretched party or not.

But, unable to put her thoughts into words, she simply glared in silent fury as Lucas lifted his cup and swallowed a mouthful of his drink, smiling his appreciation.

'Perfect.'

'It isn't exactly difficult to make a cup of coffee!'

'On the contrary, you'd be surprised how many people I've met who would prove that particular statement to be very far from the case. It's all too simple to make coffee too weak or too bitter, or just plain nasty. But you've avoided all of those problems. Aren't you having one?'

'It would keep me awake,' Georgia began but then,

suddenly assailed by the suspicion that that might be exactly what he had in mind, for his own nefarious reasons, she added hastily, 'And I don't *want* a coffee! In fact, coffee with you is the last thing on earth I want right now. And I certainly don't want to waste my time discussing how to make the perfect cup.'

Too late she saw that smile reappear and knew that, as before, he had recognised the two possible interpretations of what she had said. And, of course, being Lucas, there was one particular meaning to which he gave preference.

'So what would you rather be doing?'

I want this whole evening to be over, and to be able to go to bed and forget it! The words rose in Georgia's mind, but she knew she didn't dare to speak them, painfully aware of just how he would respond to the second half of her sentence.

'I mean, you're very prompt to let me know what you *don't* want, but give me very little clue as to what you *do*.'

'What I want—' Georgia broke in hastily, seeing the devilish gleam in his eyes and anxious to divert the conversation from the disturbing path that Lucas seemed determined to take it down. 'What I really want most in all the world is for you to drink your coffee and go. I want you to leave me in peace.'

The idea of peace suddenly seemed like something she hadn't known for a long time, certainly not since Lucas had come into her life. Was that really only four days ago?

'So you're really not bothered about this party after all? You don't want to talk things through?'

Give me patience! Georgia thought frantically, closing her eyes in an effort to draw on all her mental strength.

'What I *really* want,' she amended, through teeth clenched tight against a furious outburst, 'is for you to agree to what I've asked, decide on the arrangements and then—'

'Oh, but it's those arrangements I'm not quite clear on.'

'You're not?'

Georgia's eyes flew open, meeting the deep, slate-coloured gaze that seemed suddenly disturbingly close. He had moved, she realised, had taken a couple of steps from his position by the fireplace and come to stand beside her.

It took an effort of will to control her instinctive impulse to flinch back, unnerved by his closeness, her awareness of his size and strength overwhelming. She could smell the musky scent of his aftershave, almost feel the heat of his powerful body, and her mouth dried uncomfortably.

'But I made them perfectly clear.'

To her consternation he shook his head decisively.

'Not to me.'

'But—'

She drew in a deep breath as she struggled to remain calm. He was taunting her deliberately, she guessed, and if she rose to the bait he would have won, putting her in a much weaker position.

'What exactly didn't you understand?'

Disturbingly, even as she injected ice into her words, another less rational, more instinctive part of her brain was busy with very different thoughts. She couldn't stop it from registering how that shake of his head had disturbed the ebony sleekness of his hair, causing one dark lock to fall forward over his forehead and softening the harsh impact of his strong-boned features in a way that was somehow almost shocking.

But even more shocking was the way she had to fight against an unexpected urge to lift a hand and smooth it back.

'I just want to clear up some small points.'

As Lucas spoke his hand came out, closing over hers, making her jump like a startled cat. His smile in response to her nervous reaction was a blend of reassurance and mockery, touched with a dry amusement.

'Relax!' he soothed. 'Nothing's going to happen that you don't want. I just think that we would be more comfortable sitting down.'

The words 'relaxed' and 'comfortable' just didn't go together with this man at all, Georgia told herself. But in spite of her apprehensive feelings she found herself unable to resist the gentle but inexorable pressure on her hand that drew her with him to the settee and down beside him. *Close* beside him. Far too close for any degree of mental comfort.

'What small points?'

It was time she imposed some degree of control over the situation. He claimed that he wanted a discussion, so a discussion was all he would get.

But the lazy smile that curved Lucas's lips, the way his heavy lids had hooded his eyes, giving them a sleepily sensual look, gave the fairly definite impression that talking was not really what he had in mind.

'After all, I explained everything quite clearly.'

'Well, just run it all by me once again so that there can be no mistake.'

The only mistake in all this had to be getting tangled up with him in the first place, Georgia told herself. But, having decided that apparent co-operation was her only hope of getting through this quickly and sending him on his way, she sighed resignedly and launched once more into an account of her requirements.

'I want you to escort me to my father's party. While you're there I want you to pretend that we're…' She hunted for a suitable word, in the end deciding that the one he had used was the least emotive. 'We're a couple, and that you're crazy about me.'

'All right so far,' Lucas murmured, but his attention

was obviously not on her words. Those long fingers had released her hand and were now drifting over her head, smoothing the bright silky strands, playing with a loose tendril in a way that made her scalp tingle in response.

'Stop that!'

Freeing herself with an impatient twitch of her head, Georgia tried to continue, only to find that in fact she had made matters much worse. Lucas's rejected hand had fallen to her shoulder, where his wicked fingers stroked softly, perilously close to the exposed skin at the neck of her jacket.

'We'll travel up to Ilkley together.' A sudden dryness in her throat made the words into an embarrassing croak. 'Attend the party together.'

'Sleep together?' Lucas enquired softly, no thread of amusement lifting his voice.

'Of course not!'

'But why not?'

Suddenly, from being only vaguely attentive, his mood had changed to something much sharper as he concentrated all his attention on her in a way that made her heart lurch nervously.

'After all, if we're supposed to be crazy about each other—and I presume you want your family to think that marriage is very much on the horizon?'

A lifted eyebrow asked her to confirm or deny, but all she could manage was a silent half-nod of her head.

'Well, then, wouldn't it be expected—or at least cross someone's mind—that we might be lovers. Your sisters at least must suspect. If I was to be introduced to my sister and the man she was likely to marry, then naturally I would assume—'

'*You* would!'

Georgia had to speak, simply in order to distract herself from the way her mind was throwing up disturbing images inspired by Lucas's use of the word 'lovers' and just the thought of sleeping in the same bed as him.

Though 'sleeping' wouldn't be the operative word, she told herself. Her already unsettled mood was aggravated by the way an unwary movement brought the right side of her body into stinging contact with the hard length of his, making her pulse race frantically in reaction.

'And I suppose—' A sudden thought struck her. 'Have you got a sister?'

'No, I was simply talking theoretically.'

'Any family?'

'A father who's as crazy about speed on water as I am on land, but no one else. I'm an only child. So now that I've answered your question, why don't you do the same for mine?'

But the momentary pause had given Georgia a much-needed chance to pull herself together.

'Because yours isn't strictly relevant. You see, my mother is so very conventional—almost as old-fashioned as my father. It would never cross her mind that we could—could—'

'Fancy the pants off each other? Or do you prefer could have been intimate?' Lucas suggested, that fiendish glint lighting in his eyes again.

He was enjoying this, damn him. He was taking the same perverted pleasure in tormenting her that a cat might derive from watching a mouse run round and round in frantic circles before reaching out a lazy paw to deliver the death blow.

'Whatever! She would be bound to give us separate rooms, so you see the problem doesn't arise.'

Suddenly it was impossible to look into Lucas's face. She didn't want to meet that dark-eyed gaze or see the wicked smile hovering on his expressive mouth.

'And it's only for one night. The next day we say our goodbyes and leave.'

'Together,' Lucas put in.

'Of course together!'

He knew she was anxious to get away from the issue he had raised, and he was equally determined that it should stay in her mind.

'I said I'd provide transport there and back. We'll travel home and that will be that. It's just twenty-four hours.'

'Twenty-four hours,' Lucas echoed, giving the words an intonation that Georgia found she didn't like at all.

'Midnight to midnight, then we'll go our separate ways. We need never see each other again.'

And quite frankly she couldn't wait. The moment just couldn't come soon enough.

'So are you quite clear now?' He had to be. There was nothing else to say.

Lucas looked thoughtful.

'There's just one thing that puzzles me.'

'Oh, I don't believe it! Just what—?'

'Well, I have to admit that I don't understand why, when you've gone to all this trouble to set this up, arranging a date, telling your parents, coming out with me tonight to talk things through, you're still so insistent on keeping things strictly business. Why not make it for real, then we could have some fun?'

'We—fun!' Georgia spluttered indignantly. 'And I suppose by *fun* you mean—'

'I mean this,' Lucas drawled softly, and, leaning forward, he kissed her right on the mouth.

It wasn't a hard kiss, it couldn't even be described as forceful. In fact, it was just the softest—Georgia's whirling brain even supplied the word *tenderest*—pressure of his lips on hers. But all the same it had the effect of a much more powerful assault on her senses.

It seemed to make them all blow a fuse in one devastating moment, so that suddenly she was blind, deaf and dumb, unable to think or feel beyond the sensation of Lucas's mouth and hers and the pleasure they could create between them.

So intense was the feeling that it was as if that tiny, potent point of contact was all that held her upright. So when he finally released her by lifting his head she became limp as a puppet with all its strings cut, lolling back weakly against his supporting arm, a faint sigh escaping her.

'See.'

That sensual mouth was still only inches away from her cheek, his breath warming her skin as he gave a low, soft laugh.

'Isn't that so much better than all this strict formality? Aren't you being rather foolish to *pretend* to a passionate relationship when the real thing is yours for the taking?'

'I…' Georgia tried but the words wouldn't form, dying into an embarrassing croak.

Lucas didn't let her even try to continue, stopping her mouth with another kiss as potent as the first. This one seemed to have the power to draw her soul out of her body, making her head spin as if she was in the grip of some burning fever. She also felt hot all over, her skin flushed with warmth.

'And it can, Gia,' he whispered against her lips. 'You can have the real thing, so why settle for second-best? Why put on an act to convince your parents when we can do this—and this—?'

He gave her no time to think, no time to form a protest or even to consider whether she *wanted* to form one. Each new kiss had just a touch more intensity than the last, a shade more demand, an extra hint of passion.

Easily he drew a matching response from her, each caress waking something new, leaving her that bit more dissatisfied when it was over. All over her body his touch was sharpening a hunger, awakening a need she hadn't known she could feel.

The ivory jacket slid from her shoulders. A moment later Lucas lifted it and tossed it to one side with scant regard for the fine fabric and expensive design, and disconcertingly Georgia couldn't find it in her heart to care. No feeling of concern or conscience could break through the heated clouds that hazed her thoughts.

'And this—'

His mouth still on hers, Lucas smoothed his hands over the bare skin of her arms. One long finger traced the brocade-trimmed edges of the sleeveless waistcoat, making her shiver in response to the erotic patterns its tip drew across her sensitive flesh. Deep inside her, a primitive, very female yearning uncoiled slowly, spiralling into demanding life as his caress moved delicately over the slight swell at the sides of her breasts.

'This is a very seductive garment.'

Lucas's breath feathered over her skin, his smile a sensual touch in itself, his voice like the curl of warm smoke around her ears.

'But of course you know that. You know that it's designed to draw the eyes to one particular spot...'

A strong finger, disturbingly bronzed against her pale flesh, demonstrated exactly what he meant, sliding down the deep vee of the garment, toying with the top button.

His dark eyes fixed on the tiny pearl fastening with a concentration that was so intent that Georgia actually feared her skin might scorch under its impact. As it was, her blood heated swiftly in her veins, making her whole body colour in response to a reaction that was way beyond her control.

'I've been thinking about this all night.'

The words were just a husky whisper, stroking her senses with the same softly sure touch his hands had on her body.

'About the softness of the fabric, the delicacy of its colour, the perfume that comes up like a promise around it. But most of all about what's beneath it.'

'Lucas...'

Georgia's discomfort grew, her mouth drying painfully.

'You shouldn't!' she croaked in a feeble attempt at protest, only to see his smile grow wider.

'Oh, Gia,' he reproved gently, kissing away any further attempt from her at speech between the words. '*Shouldn't?* You and I both know that should or shouldn't don't come into this. This was inevitable from the moment we met; from the moment I looked across the hall and saw you. You can't talk of *should* when I couldn't do anything other than this, when I could no more stop it than I could keep my heart from beating.'

Warm lips were pressed against the side of her neck, just at the point where an accelerated pulse pounded wildly, betraying her response, and she felt rather than heard his low laughter against her delicate skin.

'As your heart is beating now, my lovely. Because you know it too, and that's why you wore this tempting bit of nothing. You knew it would drive me crazy, that I couldn't call myself a man if I didn't long to do this...'

The heat of his touch seared along the neckline once more. Georgia's breath stopped in her throat as his finger skimmed the top of her breasts and came to rest once more right at the very point of the vee, lying snugly in the scented valley between the soft curves.

A moment later Lucas's mouth was where his finger had been, bringing a small gasping cry from Georgia's lips as she felt the heated pressure of his kiss. The immediate response lower in her body made her feel as if the two points were joined by a burning wire along which an electrical current flared at white heat.

'Lucas!'

She had no idea how she was using his name, whether in protest or encouragement. The only thing she knew was that she had to use sound to release some of the intense pressure that was building inside her head, pulsing like a volcano about to erupt, driving out thought, driving out everything but feeling.

'Now, isn't this so much better than pretence? This way you can have your cake and eat it too, and I...'

Lucas paused, eased open the top button of her waistcoat, then pressed his lips to the opening he had made.

'I get to find out just how beautiful you really are.'

Georgia froze in a moment of exquisite delight, unable to move, scarcely able to breathe for fear she might destroy the effect his mouth was having on her.

The ripples of pleasure that radiated from the point of contact on her skin, like waves caused by a stone thrown into a pool, coursed throughout her body so that even her toes curled in response inside her fine leather shoes. And she knew that Lucas was intensely aware of her reaction as he laughed softly, easing another button from its mooring.

'Relax, darling, this is going to take a long, long time. Believe me, I have no intention of rushing things—that's not my way at all.'

And as if to prove his point he moved with deliberate slowness, one tiny inch at a time, down along the creamy path his fingers had exposed.

Georgia's body was burning up, the heat of her response making every nerve quiver. Her breasts felt heavy and tight, her nipples hardening so that they pushed against the ivory crêpe, and even the faint brush of the delicate material was almost agonisingly unbearable on the sensitised tips.

With a moaning cry she strained closer to the source of that teasing torment, closer to his hands, his mouth, to Lucas himself. Instinctively she arched her body against his, so that she felt the heated evidence of the need he too was feeling on her thigh.

The waistcoat was completely open now, its sides falling away, leaving her breasts totally exposed to those long, sure fingers that caressed and tantalised. Every touch increased the sensitivity he had awoken, building it into a spiralling agony of yearning, the pleasure mixed with a longing so very close to pain.

'I've wanted this all night—no, before that, from the moment I saw you,' Lucas whispered harshly. 'Wanted you like this—wanton, open to me, willing…' His laugh was rough and uneven. 'Oh, so willing, my lovely Gia.'

But Georgia had had enough of talk. With a murmur of complaint, she pulled him down to her again, a heartfelt sigh escaping her as she felt his mouth against hers.

Her hands tugged at the front of his shirt, pulling it open with none of the patience or finesse that he had used with her. She pushed it aside with a sigh, convulsing in uncontrollable delight at the sensation as the dark curls of hair on his chest rubbed in erotic abrasion against the erect points of her breasts.

'Please—please—' It was a litany of need on her tongue, the words escaping involuntarily, coming from somewhere deep inside, not registering on her brain at all.

'Please, what, Gia?' Lucas teased, his own voice thickened with desire. 'Tell me what you want and I'll give it to you. Is it this?'

His hands cupped both her breasts, lifting their soft fullness towards his face so that for a moment the hard plane of his cheek lay against their white smoothness.

'Or this?'

Encouraged by her response, the hectic fire in her eyes, he trailed his tongue over one breast, moving towards the taut nipple, circling it with tormenting deliberation before acceding to her incoherent demand and letting his mouth close over the sensitised peak. He sucked softly at first, then with an increasing force that brought a sound that was almost a scream of delight from her lips.

'What else? Where else would you like me to pleasure you? Here?'

He turned his attention to the other breast, producing

sensations that had her writhing in tormented ecstasy, unable to bear any more and yet fearful that he might stop.

'Or here...?'

His hands had found the fastening on her trousers, sliding down the zip so that now his hard fingers slipped inside the creamy lace beneath and closed over the very heart of her femininity.

'You only have to ask, sweetheart. Just say the word. I can't deny you anything. I could never say no to anything you wanted, never...'

Never say no. The words slashed through the blazing passion in Georgia's brain like a blade of ice, dousing the flames in a rush of cold, hard reality.

Never say no. 'Georgie, *no one* says no to Lucas Mallory...' Kelly's face swam before her eyes; Kelly's voice was in her head, driving the last vestiges of that wanton madness before it as a broken reed is washed away by a tumbling river current.

'Mallory's Moppets, we're known as... There's another, less flattering term for the others... The proverbial one night stand...'

'*No!*'

It was a cry of shock, of disgust, of sheer blind panic and disbelief at what she had almost let happen. The violence of her rejection gave her a strength she hadn't known she possessed as she pushed at the hard wall of his chest, wrenching her body to one side at the same moment so that she was off the settee and on her feet before either of them quite realised what was happening.

'No, no, no!' she cried, still swaying with the force of her reaction. 'This isn't— I won't—'

'What the hell—?'

Lucas's face, still flushed with desire, turned to her in confusion. Eyes like burnished jet blazed in their deep-set sockets, and a terrible, savage violence was etched onto his features.

'Gia—' It was a dangerous, ominous sound, the warning implicit in it making her shiver convulsively and hold up her hands in a fearful, defensive gesture. 'What—?'

But then, abruptly, he seemed to pull himself up sharply. Georgia watched in stunned disbelief as, like some amazing special effect in a film, his whole expression, the set of his features, every inch of his body underwent a total transformation.

If he had suddenly pulled on a mask that covered his face he couldn't have looked so impossibly different, so unlike the man of moments before. It was almost as if another man stood before her, one she didn't know, and one who, impossibly, unbelievably, smiled at her with unexpected gentleness.

'Gia, what is all this about? This isn't how it's meant to be. Come back...'

'No!' Hands still outstretched, Georgia took a hasty step backwards when it seemed he would get to his feet and come after her. 'No, there isn't any "meant to be". I'm not coming back—not now, not ever. You—'

'Just what has brought about this sudden attack of nerves?' Lucas demanded, cutting in on her harshly. 'You said there was no other man.'

'There isn't, but—'

'Then why play games? There's no need.'

'I'm not playing games! This isn't what I meant to happen.'

'No?' Dark cynicism coiled around the word as he flung it at her coldly. 'Oh, come on, Gia, be honest with yourself at least. This is what you had in mind from the start. Why else did you "buy" me? Why invite me here?'

The arrogance of his statement, the cold edge to the questions hit home like a blow to her head. For a moment it was almost as if she was no longer in her body but looking down at herself as she had been just seconds before. She could see the flush in her cheeks, the bright hair pulled loose and falling in tangled disarray around her shoulders, her lipstick kissed off, her clothes...

Georgia closed her eyes in an attempt to drive away the appalling image but it persisted, reminding her of how she had been—so wanton, so dishevelled, so totally out of control.

'No!'

This wasn't how she had wanted it to be at all! It had nothing to do with the scheme she had planned.

Somehow, during the evening, the balance she had aimed for had shifted dangerously, the reins being snatched from her grasp. Now it was as if a spirited horse that before had been only barely under control had been given its head and was running away with her, careering down the road at an increasingly dangerous speed.

'No?' The single syllable was injected with as much scepticism as he could possibly manage.

'No,' Georgia repeated desperately. 'This isn't what I want from you.'

Lucas raked one hand through his dark hair. 'OK, I'm sorry. I took things too fast.'

This was worse than ever. 'No! No, you didn't—'

'Then what?'

The dark edge to his words, the warning that his patience was wearing thin had her rushing into nervous response.

She pulled the edges of her gaping waistcoat round her and held them tight, unable to find the co-ordination to fasten the buttons. It was a struggle to ignore the agonising sensation of the material rubbing against her tender, aching breasts as she tried to find a way to put her feelings into words.

'You didn't take it "too fast," because that implies that if you had taken things more slowly it would have been all right, that at some point I would have conceded and welcomed your advances. Well, you couldn't be more wrong!'

How she wished she could control her voice. It came and went like the sound of a radio that was subject to the most appalling static, and his sardonic lifting of one dark eyebrow in an expression of cynical disbelief only made matters worse.

'*I don't want this at all!* Not fast or slow, not now, not ever! Never, never, *never*! Got that?'

'Loud and clear.'

The bitterly mocking salute with which Lucas accompanied the words only emphasised the terrible coldness of his voice, and she couldn't meet his eyes, knowing that they would be cold and bleak as any of the Arctic wastes.

'Loud and clear,' he repeated, even more harshly. 'So now I suppose it's back to strictly business, is it? You're sure that is what you want?'

The trouble was that Georgia was no longer so sure. Her original plan, with its careful safety net of 'strictly business' seemed to lie in pieces at her feet, together with the shattered remnants of her ability to control what was happening. She had no idea how to put it back together again, or even if she wanted to.

Right now, she could barely summon the energy to think. Her whole body ached terribly, protesting painfully at the loss of the pleasure and satisfaction it had yearned for and which had been so abruptly denied it.

'I'm perfectly sure.' A control that matched his made her words coldly clear and precise. 'Strictly business is exactly what I want.'

'Then you'll have to forgive me if I can't agree to abide by the terms of our original agreement. You see, circumstances have changed considerably, and the way I feel about things can no longer be confined to the narrow definition of a business partnership.'

I bet they can't, Georgia thought bitterly. His voice

might be every bit as cool as his reputation made him out to be, but the still uneven tenor of his breathing, the wild glitter in his eyes warned her that his apparent control was only a thin veneer on the surface of a boiling volcano.

The thought of the fiercely primitive passion that blazed underneath that apparently civilised surface made her blood run cold. Now she knew how true Kelly's words had been, recognising that no one said no to Lucas Mallory for two very distinct reasons.

One was that his seductive technique was every bit as lethal as her friend had claimed. But the second, and more worrying one, was that if anyone was fool enough to resist that technique then they had to face the possible consequences.

'And that being so,' Lucas continued, in a voice that was so cold it almost froze her skin as the words formed in the air, 'I have to withdraw from our agreement.'

'What?'

For a couple of stunned seconds she could only stand and stare.

'What do you mean? Are you telling me that if I won't sleep with you, you won't help me out?'

'That's not exactly how I would have phrased it...'

'But it's what you meant! So why don't you just come out and say it?'

No matter how carefully he might have put it, how delicately this Lucas, this apparently civilised, controlled man, might have danced around the edges of his real meaning, the bottom line was the same. His basic message—his *very* basic message—was just as she had known from the start.

'All right, I admit I want you. I want you so much that there is no way I'm prepared to go through with this farce.'

'Well, you don't have to!' Unexpected pain made her voice high and sharp, tearing into his words. 'Because if that's the way you think—' she wouldn't honour the things he had said with the description of feeling '—then the deal's off, once and for all! I can't bear the sight of you, and I never want to see you again. I want you out of my house now, and out of my life!'

She was physically pushing at him as she spoke, forcing him to his feet and towards the door. The simple fact that he went unresistingly drove home just how little he wanted to stay.

But when they reached the front door he turned suddenly.

'What will you do about the party?'

It was the last thing she had expected, the last thing she cared about. Right now, the party was the least of her worries.

'To hell with the party! I'll find someone else.'

'There's barely a week left.'

'I'll find someone else,' she reiterated through clenched teeth. 'Anyone has to be better than you. I wouldn't want you now if you were the last man on earth.'

It was only when the words were out that she realised how, unconsciously, she had almost echoed his own scathing comment to her on the night of the auction.

'Fine.' She would have sworn that it was impossible for his voice to get any colder, but somehow he managed it. 'See you around.'

'Not if I see you first!'

But when she had slammed the door in his face, was leaning against it, breathing heavily, the burning mist slowly cleared from her mind, bringing her hard up against reality. Suddenly she was forced to question whether the emotions that had seethed inside her head had simply been the blazing anger that she had first thought.

Wasn't it true that that simple anger had been complicated by other emotions—emotions that were much more disturbing to her peace of mind? It was something so threatening to her mental equilibrium that her mind reeled away from even considering the implications of it.

The only thing she dared to admit to herself was that the one thing that *hadn't* motivated her was the thought that had come straight to Lucas's mind. Disappointment at the thought of missing the party had been the furthest thing from her head at the time.

Which was perhaps the most worrying thing of all.

CHAPTER SEVEN

'IT'S the big day on Saturday, isn't it? Your father's party.'

Kelly's blue eyes lit up from inside and her smile was wide and bright, as if she was the one looking forward to the event.

'Are you all ready? Got the dress?'

'No.'

Try as she might, Georgia couldn't produce a smile in response to her friend's excitement. The thought of the party and the trip home it involved had been sticking in her mind like a thorn for days now, growing more and more uncomfortable with each hour that passed since the moment she had closed the door on Lucas.

'I mean, yes, I've got the clothes and everything.'

The outfit she planned to wear was hanging in her wardrobe; the present had been bought and wrapped. In all ways but one, everything was in order.

'But I can't say I'm looking forward to going up to Yorkshire on my own.'

'On your own?' Kelly echoed, a puzzled frown creasing her forehead, and she pushed back the wave of blonde hair that had fallen over her face. 'But I thought that was all under control.'

'Kelly, you of all people should know that Lucas Mallory is not someone who could ever be described as being "under control"!' Georgia returned feelingly and her friend nodded.

'What happened? I mean, you had it all mapped out. The auction—'

'The auction went fine.' Georgia sighed, recalling how she and Kelly had planned it all, almost giggling like schoolgirls at the thought of turning the tables on the man who had treated the other girl so badly. It had seemed such a good idea at the time, using him simply as a sort of stage prop, the type of decorative accessory that he obviously regarded women as being. 'But after that things didn't work out as I'd anticipated.'

Understatement of the year, she told herself in the privacy of her thoughts. *Nothing* had gone as she'd expected.

'In what way?'

'What do you think?'

'Georgie! He didn't pounce?'

'You don't have to sound so surprised!' Georgia retorted, piqued by the note in her friend's voice. 'I mean, you of all people should know what he's like.'

'I suppose I do.' Kelly was studying the sheaf of papers in her hands, shuffling through them abstractedly.

'But I told him exactly where he got off.'

'So that's an end to it all?'

'That's right,' Georgia confirmed, adding hastily, 'Not that it ever *began* in the first place. And I can't say I'm worried. There's no way Lucas Mallory would have fitted in with my plans. Are these the wallpaper samples for the Finnegan house? Let's have a look at them.'

Who was she trying to kid? she was forced to ask herself on her way home that night. Lucas would have fitted in perfectly. He would have been everything she had wanted, and she had no chance of finding anyone to replace him.

Oh, she had tried. She'd racked her brains, gone through her address book with a fine-toothed comb, but no one had come to mind—no one suitable anyway.

'Face it,' she told herself aloud as she parked her car.

'When you've had Lucas Mallory and lost him, who could possibly hope to take his place?'

But then, realising just what she had said, she shook her head frantically, trying to rid herself of the impact the words could have on her if she actually let them sink in.

She was only fooling herself anyway. She had never, ever *had* Lucas in any way whatsoever. Her foolish belief that she had been in control at any point had just been an illusion. Lucas had played things by his own rules from the start, and he was the one who had been in the driving seat both literally and metaphorically.

'Good evening, Gia.'

The quiet voice came from behind her, startling her so that she jumped like a scalded cat, whirling round, the door key falling from her hand and landing on the pavement with a clatter.

'Steady!' With a smooth, graceful movement Lucas bent and scooped it up, inserting it in the lock and turning it firmly before continuing with a touch of dry amusement, 'You really are on edge, aren't you? Anyone would think you had a guilty conscience.'

'On the contrary!' Georgia snapped, her movements jerky and unsettled as she adjusted, quite unnecessarily, the jacket of her plum coloured suit, brushing a couple of imaginary specks from its straight skirt. '*Anyone* would react in just the same way if you crept up behind them like that!'

'I didn't *creep*,' Lucas reproved. 'I made enough noise to be heard under normal circumstances, but you were so lost in your thoughts that you didn't notice.'

'Problems at work,' Georgia improvised hastily, irrationally fearful that he might actually be able to see into her thoughts and realise what had kept her so preoccupied.

It didn't help that she had spent the past few days trying to forget about the physical impact he had had on her. She had almost convinced herself that she was exaggerating, that no man could be *that* attractive, *that* imposing. But now, with him standing before her, dark and devastating in another of those superbly tailored business suits, she knew that she could never have succeeded.

Lucas was all male, vitally and forcefully alive, and the aura of success and money that he projected without any apparent effort served only to enhance and increase the sensual impact of his physical presence.

'I see. Poor Gia, you're really not having a very successful time, are you? And it's the party on Saturday.'

'I know that perfectly well, so if you've just come to gloat then you can take yourself off again!'

'Gloat!' Mockery gleamed in his eyes, contradicting the assumed note of pain in the word. 'My dear Gia, what an appalling opinion you have of me.'

'Then perhaps you'll enlighten me as to precisely why I'm being honoured by this unexpected visit?'

'Certainly. Though I'm sure you can guess that I came to find out if you'd found a replacement.'

So she'd been right about the gloating after all. Unless...

Her thought process stopped dead as an idea struck home with the force of a blow to her head. He couldn't actually be prepared to offer to go with her after all, could he?

No, it wasn't possible, she told herself, struggling to ignore the sudden quickening of her heart at the thought. She'd told herself that he was the last man she wanted to be with, but the fact remained that he was the one who would have the most effect on her father.

'Of course I have! You don't think you're the only man in the world?'

'Who?' Lucas demanded, knocking her off balance for a moment.

'Oh—Peter Dawlish.'

She pulled a name out of the air, picking one of the other men at the auction, hoping he wouldn't know who she meant, and knew she had failed when she saw the look of scorn that crossed his face.

'Dawlish!' he echoed contemptuously. 'And do you think that your father will be impressed to see you in the company of a twice-divorced *fishmonger*?'

'He's a lovely man…' Her voice was as weak as she knew her argument to be.

'And from what I've heard your papa eats men like him for breakfast.' Abruptly Lucas changed tack, wrong-footing her again. 'What are you wearing?'

'Wearing?'

'To the party!'

'It's none of your—'

But some flicker of her eyes up towards the window of her bedroom must have betrayed her.

'Upstairs, is it?' he asked, pushing the door open and moving past her.

His behaviour was just too much.

'Now, wait a minute!'

But Lucas ignored her outburst, taking the stairs two at a time and finding her bedroom with disturbing ease. He flung open the door, dark eyes going straight to the black tuxedo-style jacket and trousers that hung from the wardrobe mirror.

'*No!*' he declared adamantly.

'No?' Georgia was beginning to feel like a dazed parrot repeating everything he said. 'What do you mean no?'

'You are not wearing that!'

'What's it got to do with you, whatever I wear?' Georgia demanded. 'And just what is wrong with it?' She'd spent a fortune on that suit.

'What's *wrong* with it? Just look.' Lucas ignored the first half of her question as a contemptuous wave of one hand indicated the offending garment. 'Gia, you don't have to ask; you *know* what's wrong with it. It's a man's outfit.'

'But Joely…' She named the auctioneer at the charity dinner '…she looks stunning in—'

'Joely isn't you! She's a beanpole. Hell and damnation, woman!' he exploded. 'Do you want to deny everything that's special about you? You're a woman! A beautiful, desirable, very sexy woman! You have fabulous legs, long, slender arms, and…'

His eyes dropped from her face quite deliberately and his voice had a husky roughness to it when he continued. 'And a stunning cleavage that needs no artifice to enhance it. *This*—' Once more he indicated the suit with a dismissive gesture. 'This will simply conceal them all. And with you in that and me in a dinner jacket we'll look like brothers. You just can't be serious!'

'Never more so…'

Her words died in her throat as she realised just what his words implied.

'You said—with you in…'

'In a dinner jacket,' Lucas completed for her when her voice failed her again. 'I take it that it *is* going to be formal?'

Georgia could only nod, swallowing hard to ease the painful tightness in her throat.

'Does—does this mean—? Are you coming?'

Lucas's nod was swift and curt, his eyes hooded and unreadable, no emotion showing in his face.

'But *why*?'

And how did she feel about that? She tried to tell herself that it was relief that pitched her voice so high, but, although it was partly true, there was also much more than that. Her head held a tangle of feelings she couldn't begin to sort out.

'I couldn't live with my conscience otherwise,' Lucas returned flatly. 'You paid well over the odds for a partner for this damned party, and the charity benefited because of that. I agreed to help them, and if I don't fulfil my part of the bargain I'm not playing fair by them.'

Playing fair by the charity, not by her, Georgia noted on a twist of bitterness. It was what she should have expected, much less than she might have hoped for, but it was all she was going to get. She told herself she should be satisfied with that, but, strangely, found that such a feeling was beyond her.

Because somehow, in the time since Lucas had walked out on her, the problem of needing an escort for the party had become newly important in a way that was so very different from the attitude with which she had started out on this.

In the past few days, the pendulum had swung away from her concern that her partner should simply be a man who could impress her father and towards a new, more complicated idea. It had now become vital to her that *Lucas* and he alone should be that partner, in a way that had nothing to do with any possible effect on her father.

'I don't want you there!'

Perversity made her say it, the need to stand up to him so as to make sure that he didn't simply trample all over her. That and the fact that she felt too dangerously vulnerable, too emotionally off balance to consider the possible full implications of her recent realisation.

'I'd rather go a—'

'Tough,' was Lucas's bluntly unyielding comment. 'As I said, you paid for me so I shall have to deliver.'

'On the same terms as before, then?' The effort to control her voice's tendency to quaver made it harder and colder than she had intended.

'Terms?'

Something in his emotionless tone, the steely glint in his eyes sent a shiver down her spine, so that she had to force herself to go on.

'Strictly business.'

For a disturbing second the generous mouth thinned dangerously, then, even as Georgia swallowed hard in nervous apprehension, Lucas appeared to relax again.

But she had let herself off the hook too soon, she realised as he turned on her a smile of such frighteningly obvious insincerity that her blood chilled in her veins at the thought of what lay behind it.

'Strictly business, Georgia. Midnight to midnight,' he drawled lazily. 'You'll get what you paid for. After that, I reserve the right to alter the terms of our arrangement as and when it suits me.'

The grey eyes challenged her to protest, but Georgia knew with a sense of despair that she was weak enough to accept any terms as long as he was at her side when she came face to face with her father.

'Agreed?'

'Agreed.' Georgia nodded coolly. 'I only wanted twenty-four hours, nothing more.'

Now what had she done? But even as she asked herself the question the look of black anger that had prompted it—if anger it had been—had vanished after only a split second, leaving his face blank and calm once more. A moment later his mood had changed yet again.

'But this will have to go.'

Swinging away from her, he snatched the tuxedo suit from the hanger and tossed it carelessly into a corner of the room.

'Lucas! That cost me a small fortune!'

'I'll replace it with something much better; something that will make you look like a million dollars so that even your so-pretty sisters are thrown into the shade.'

'You don't have to put on the act yet!' Georgia protested, unable to know how to respond to the extravagant compliments he was tossing out so casually. 'The day of the party will be fine.'

'How do you know it's an act?' Lucas demanded,

leaving her at a loss for an answer. 'Now, about this dress...'

'I only have tomorrow free to go shopping.'

'We'll get it tonight.' Lucas dismissed her protest with an arrogant wave of his hand.

'But will anywhere be open? It's well after seven.'

'I know someone who'll help. There'll be no problem. Get your coat.'

'Well, admit it. I was right.'

Georgia stared at her reflection in the mirror, frankly unable to believe her eyes.

'You were right,' she said slowly. 'Absolutely right.'

He had promised to find her a dress that made her look like a million dollars, and he had delivered just that. She had been doubtful at first, then stunned when he had driven her to this exclusive boutique.

'You look wonderful.' The manageress, a slim, elegant brunette of around thirty who had been introduced as Vanessa, came to stand beside her now, smiling at her in the mirror. 'Is it for a special occasion?'

Georgia nodded, still staring at her reflection. The dress was a simple sheath in a rich cream silk, its colour a perfect foil for the brightness of her hair, making her eyes look huge and surprisingly dark. Its sleek lines clung lovingly to every curve of her body, ending just above the knee, and the effect of severity was lightened by the way that the bodice was composed almost entirely of heavy lace through which the rose tones of her skin gleamed softly.

'Well, at least you look like a woman.'

Lucas's words drove the contented smile from Georgia's mouth, tightening her muscles suddenly, and when her gaze went to his face, the tension inside her tightened another notch.

His comment might have sounded casual, throwaway, almost, but that was not the message his eyes were giving her. Something primitive burned in their ebony depths, flaring into an uninhibited sensuality as he subjected her to a lingering survey from top to toe. The scrutiny was so intense she almost expected to see the beautiful fabric of the dress scorch along the path his eyes had taken.

'Perhaps not—' she began, but Lucas shook his head adamantly.

'No dress, no escort,' he murmured, so quietly that Vanessa did not catch the words. But behind the softness of his tone was a backbone of unyielding obduracy that she knew she would be wise to heed. Besides, it was a beautiful dress...

'We'll take it, then.'

The knowledge that Lucas had seen the weakening on her face sent a shiver down her spine, and she realised just how closely he had been watching her reaction.

'We'll take it,' she confirmed, her voice not quite steady, because somehow accepting the dress seemed to imply so much more than just letting Lucas buy her something to wear.

A short time later, with the dress carefully wrapped in layers of tissue and folded into an elegant gold box, Vanessa saw them to the door.

'Have a wonderful time wearing it,' she told Georgia.

'I will. And thank you for opening up for us.'

They had arrived just as the manageress had been leaving for the night, but she had unlocked the door without protest and set herself to selecting suitable outfits as easily as if it had been early afternoon.

'Oh, that's no bother,' Vanessa assured her. 'Anything to help Lucas.'

And she meant it too, Georgia realised. The look Vanessa turned in his direction was soft and warm, as if a light had switched on behind her eyes. Seeing it, Georgia's heart gave a nasty little jerk of reaction, her gasp of shock having to be swallowed down hastily as she recognised just what it was that she was feeling.

Could she? Was it possible that she could really be *jealous* of Vanessa and her obviously warm relationship with Lucas? The thought shook her to the very core of her being.

'So now what?' Lucas slid into the driving seat of his car and turned to her as he spoke. 'Where would you like to eat?'

Food was the last thing on her mind. If she was perfectly honest, the only thing she wanted was to go home, run a warm, relaxing bath and have a very early night. Not because she was tired—the suspicion that sleep would be hard to come by was strong in her mind—but because she was urgently in need of some hours' peace and quiet in order to come to terms with the surprising developments of the day.

But Lucas had bought her a very expensive meal some days before, and an even more costly dress today.

'Well, I do owe you a dinner. But I'm not exactly dressed for anywhere too posh.'

'You'll be fine for what I have in mind,' Lucas assured her, swinging the car out from the kerb.

When they drew to a halt again a short time later, Georgia couldn't believe her eyes. Blinking hard, she looked again, but everything was still the same.

'Fish and chips!' Her incredulity rang in her voice. Somehow the sophisticated Lucas Mallory and the simple food didn't go together.

'Perfect when you're really hungry.' Lucas nodded. 'And, believe me, I'm starving. Do you want to eat in or out?'

'Oh, out!' Already the savoury smell was drifting through the car's open windows, making her mouth water. 'It's years since I ate chips from the paper. But I warn you, they had better be good! You're dealing with a real connoisseur here, someone who firmly believes the best fish and chips can only be found in the North.'

'Food snob!' Lucas returned drily. 'But I don't think you'll be disappointed.'

'You were right,' Georgia sighed contentedly some time later as she swallowed the last tasty morsel. 'They *were* good. I haven't had a pig-out like that in ages, and eating them from the bag was like being a kid again.'

'Your papa let you do things like that?'

'Well, no, not often,' Georgia admitted in response to the note of surprise in the question. 'It wasn't the done thing for the Harding girls to be seen behaving like that. But occasionally, just once in a while, I rebelled.'

'Is that a fact?'

'You don't believe me? Oh, all right, I admit most of the time I did as I was told—more than that. I tried to be the son my father wanted, to share in everything that interested him. The hours I spent watching endless sports programmes or learning about Antarctic exploration and other things that fascinated him.'

'And did it work?'

'No...' Sadly Georgia shook her head, staring fixedly out at the street as she fought against the pressure of tears in her eyes. 'He'd just say that such things weren't suitable subjects for girls, that if I'd been a boy—'

She bit off the rest of the sentence, knowing she couldn't say it without giving in to her feelings.

'But I don't suppose even a precious son would have been allowed to eat chips like this. And perhaps he was right. After all, now I'm covered in grease.' She licked one fingertip, where traces of salt and vinegar still lingered. 'I...'

The words died on her tongue as she looked up to see Lucas's eyes on her, disturbingly deep and dark, following the movement of her hand and then lingering, staring fixedly at her mouth.

His expression was so full of raw need that her heart

leapt nervously, and she had to swallow hastily to relieve
the aching dryness of her throat. Her tongue slid out to
lick her lips, stilling hastily as she saw his grey-eyed
gaze follow the betraying movement.

She had never been so aware of his physical closeness
in the confined space of the car. Every sense seemed
newly alert to the width of his shoulders, the strength of
his profile against the window. The tang of some cologne tantalised her nostrils, mixing with the deeper,
much more personal scent of his body.

'Do—do you have a tissue or something that I could
wipe my fingers on?' she managed, her voice croaking
awkwardly, her heart beating so fast that she was sure
he must hear its rapid pulse in the silence of the night.

'What?' With an obvious effort he came back to himself, as if from a long, long way away. 'Oh, yes. Here.'

He pulled a handkerchief from his pocket and held it
out to her. Georgia stared at the immaculate white linen
in some dismay.

'I can't use that!'

Lucas's shrug dismissed her protest.

'It'll wash. I'll see to it as soon as I get home.'

Home. The word buzzed inside Georgia's head, bringing with it ideas previously unconsidered.

'Where *is* home, Lucas? Do you realise I hardly know
anything about you or your family?' The thought had
never crossed her mind before; Lucas had always
seemed so complete in himself.

The swift, sidelong glance he turned on her had a
sudden coolness that made her want to shiver, as if the
temperature in the car had dropped by several degrees.

'I didn't think such things came under the heading of
"Strictly Business".'

'But I *should* have asked.'

Her conscience was uncomfortable at the thought, her
unease aggravated by the realisation of just how much
she wanted to know about him. But she couldn't let him

see that. To do so would certainly be to breach the terms of their agreement, and so she forced herself to put a controlled note of reason into her words as she continued.

'And besides, if we're to be a couple then I should know just as much about you as you should about me.'

Something had changed again. Just as earlier in the evening she had had the feeling that she had inadvertently trodden on his toes, metaphorically speaking, so she felt now that once again something had caused him to step back, withdraw from her, mentally if not physically.

'Ask away.'

'I'm sorry.' The total lack of emotion in his words made her say it. 'I should have—'

'There's no *should* about it, Gia. After all, I doubt if a slave owner in ancient Rome would have taken the time or trouble to find out about the background or family of their latest purchase.'

'But we both know—'

'Know what?' A lifted eyebrow gave added emphasis to the sardonic enquiry. 'What is it that you're so sure we both know about our arrangement?'

'Well, that this slave business has nothing to do with our relationship.'

'I thought it had everything to do with it, that it was the reason why we couldn't have a *relationship*.' He emphasised the word in a way that made Georgia flinch inside. 'After all, you were the one who laid down terms, insisted we keep our distance.'

'Oh, I see.' At last she thought she understood the way his mind was working. 'You don't want me to invade your privacy, is that it?'

'If you think that, then you really don't see at all.'

'Then tell me!'

His silence in response to her outburst shook her. Not only did she not understand it, but it had a worrying quality about it—a sense of waiting, of *calculation* that she didn't know how to explain or react to. At last Lucas moved, raking one strong hand through his hair.

'What is it you want to know? Let me see. How old am I? Thirty-five. Am I married? No, and no commitments either. Brothers or sisters? Not one. Parents? My father, who I believe I have mentioned, and my mother, who died when I was six. Since—'

'Six!' Georgia couldn't hold back a cry of shock and sympathy for the child he had been then. 'Oh, Lucas!'

'It was ages ago, Gia, and she'd been ill for a long time. To be perfectly honest, I don't remember that time all that well, and just lately I've had the happy experience of acquiring a wonderful stepmother.'

'Your father got married again?'

Lucas nodded. 'To Ruth. She's twenty years younger than him, barely five years older than me, but she knows how to handle him—both of us. What else? My racing career has been public knowledge for years, and you know what I do now. Leisurewise, I like to swim and—'

'Oh, stop it!'

Georgia couldn't take any more. When she'd said she wanted to know more about him she hadn't anticipated this cold, emotionless listing of facts, as if on some very businesslike CV.

'What's wrong, Gia?'

The look he turned on her made her feel as if she was some sort of specimen under a microscope, and not a very pleasant one at that.

'This is the sort of thing you'll need to be aware of if your family ask questions. And, believe me, it's nothing more than most of my business associates know.'

Which made it perfectly plain exactly what he was doing, just in case she had ever been in doubt. It shouldn't bother her, in fact it was what she'd said she wanted, but that wasn't at all the way she felt.

'I preferred it when we agreed to ask questions turn

and turn about,' she said. 'That way I'd get to find out the things that really intrigue me—like why did you choose to support that particular charity? I mean, a premature baby unit isn't—'

'A friend of mine's baby was born more than seven weeks premature. She was already having a very tough time, and if she had lost the baby as well, it would have destroyed her. Saint Jo's saved the child's life, and very probably hers into the bargain.'

It wasn't at all what she had expected, so much so that it reduced her to stunned silence—a fact that Lucas took advantage of very swiftly.

'My turn. So, tell me, why the Ice Maiden?'

'What?' If she hadn't already been slightly off balance she might have handled it better. 'It's none of your business!'

'I'm making it my business. You said you wanted answers to the really intriguing questions, and so do I.' It had the ring of an ultimatum about it. 'So, come on, why have you been labelled the Ice Maiden?'

He would persist until he got an answer, she knew. The hard, unyielding set of his features told her that.

'It was a man called Jason who started it,' she began reluctantly. 'I'd been out with him a couple of times and he was pressing me to take our relationship further. I wasn't interested; he persisted. In the end it all got rather nasty, and he started to spread rumours about me—telling people I was frigid.'

'Redeeming his reputation at the expense of yours. Nice guy,' Lucas muttered harshly, then, at the movement of her head, he frowned. 'Why are you looking at me like that?'

Georgia was beyond telling him anything but the truth. 'Because, quite frankly, I expected a very different reaction.'

'That I'd side with the selfish bastard? Why? Simply

because I'm male and so is he? What an appallingly low opinion you have of me.'

'I did make matters worse by freezing out anyone else who wanted to see me at that time,' Georgia admitted hastily, needing to be scrupulously honest. 'You see, I'd just set up on my own, and I really needed to concentrate on building my reputation, establishing contacts—'

She broke off in surprise when he nodded understanding.

'You believe me?'

'And why not?'

'They didn't—those other men.'

'Ah, but they didn't know about your relationship with your father and how much you wanted to prove yourself to him. If they had, then they'd have understood just how important it was to you to make a success of your business in order to show him.'

Had she told him that or had he simply deduced it from the things she had told him? Georgia wondered, thinking back over the conversation they had had at the restaurant and trying to recall precisely what she had said.

'And, besides…' Lucas let the word trail off so that she glanced at him curiously, catching the faint smile that curved the corners of his mouth.

'Besides—what?' she demanded, and immediately wished she hadn't as that smile grew, becoming once more the unholy grin she recognised from their earlier meetings.

'*I'm* well aware of the fact that you're not in the least frigid. In fact I have irrefutable evidence to the contrary.'

He twisted in his seat, laying one long hand against her cheek, its palm lightly cupping the fine line of her jaw, holding her wide hazel eyes with his own dark gaze.

'Evidence?' Georgia croaked, a shiver of awareness shaking her as that smile grew still wider.

Right now, those amazing eyes really were black, she

thought hazily. Black as jet, without a trace of grey even at the outer edges of the iris.

'Firsthand evidence,' Lucas murmured. 'You forget that I know exactly what you look like when you come alive in a man's arms. That I've seen how the colour rises in these pale cheeks, how your mouth softens…'

His voice had deepened, becoming softly seductive, holding her transfixed as his face came slowly nearer and nearer, his mouth only inches away from hers.

'I've watched those clear bright eyes haze over with passion, heard your voice change and become husky with desire. If this Jason couldn't rouse you, then he must be all sorts of a fool as well as an insensitive brute. You're no more frigid than Mount Vesuvius, my lovely, and with the right man's touch…'

But that was just too much.

'And I suppose that by "the right man" you mean yourself?'

Georgia wrenched herself free of the trance in which he had held her, watching with distinctly ambiguous feelings as Lucas's head went back, his eyes narrowing swiftly. Her stomach lurched uncomfortably as the wide mouth that only seconds before had been sensually inviting thinned to a cold, hard line.

'Perhaps you'd like to compare notes with Jason, give him a few pointers? You could let him know just what's wrong with his technique.'

'No *technique*, Georgia.' His voice was as cold as his expression, and the use of her full name warned of the dangers of provoking him any further—a warning she refused to heed.

'No, of course not!' she flung at him, making the words as satirical as was possible when her heart was pounding high up in her throat. '*You* are just so totally irresistible that you only have to touch a woman and she falls into your hands like a ripe little plum.'

The problem was that he *was*; at least as far as she

was concerned. The way her heart was racing now, the pounding beat of her pulse thudding inside her head and driving out reasonable thought, told her how weak she was where he was concerned. And she had thought that *Kelly* had behaved foolishly!

If that was the case, then how could she describe her own stupidity? After all, she was well aware of Lucas's reputation, one he had made no attempt to deny, and she had Kelly's experience to act as evidence and warning. Yet she had still fallen prey to the smooth, practised skill with which he had turned on that potently seductive technique. And it *was* a technique, no matter how he tried to deny it!

'If the cap fits,' Lucas murmured, incensing her further.

'I'd like to go home now!' she declared. 'Straight home! And, *no*, I have no intention of inviting you in for coffee or—'

She had almost added 'or anything else!', but swallowed the foolish words down hastily, knowing them to be dangerously provocative.

Another of those swift sidelong glances was slanted in her direction as Lucas moved away from her to turn the key in the ignition.

'Did I suggest any such thing?' he asked, the mocking edge to his voice leaving her in no doubt that he had been well aware of just what had been in her mind. 'And don't you think you would do better to wait until there's a real threat of danger before you start lashing out?'

Unable to think of a suitably crushing retort, Georgia simply subjected him to a fulminating glare and remained obstinately silent for the short time it took to reach the street in which she lived. As soon as the car drew to a halt she turned to the door, reaching speedily for the handle.

'Just a minute.' Lucas's cool tones stopped her dead. What now? Reluctantly she turned to face him.

'What is it?'

'Don't look like that.' To her astonishment and embarrassment, Lucas actually laughed. 'I'm not about to leap on you and kiss you senseless.'

She wouldn't put it past him, Georgia thought, fighting against her body's instinctively excited response to the thought of being kissed senseless by this particular man.

'What is it?' she asked again, this time through gritted teeth.

'I just wanted to know if you realise that you're actually playing right into your father's hands with the approach you've planned.'

'I'm what?' Her very different intonation revealed her consternation.

'By taking me with you to this party you're telling your father that he's right, that without a man at your side you're nothing, not worth his time or attention. You're declaring that all you've achieved in starting up your own business, the success you've made of your life doesn't count, and that what counts least of all is the fact that you're a woman.'

Georgia knew that her mouth had actually fallen open in shock. If she thought he had surprised her earlier, then *this* seemed to spark off an explosion inside her brain.

'I—' If she was honest, she had never looked at it that way before, had never thought beyond the fact that she wanted her father to love her and be proud of her. 'I don't see how—' she began.

'Can't you see that this way you're still trailing round him like you did when you were a little girl, looking for Daddy's attention, his approval? I never took you for a coward, Gia.'

'I'm not!' But something of what he had said struck home, putting an unwanted quaver into her denial.

'Then don't let him win. Stand up to him.'

'It's all very well—' Georgia began but Lucas ignored her.

'You're not a little girl any more. You're a fully grown, independent woman. Be yourself. That way you can beat him at his own game.'

Was it possible? Georgia asked herself. Could that really be the way to handle things? Nothing had worked so far, but then she had always followed much the same path, had always tried to please.

'You could be right,' she said slowly. 'I never looked at it that way before.'

Acting on an impulse too strong to resist, she leaned forward and pressed a light kiss on the hard plane of his cheek.

'Thank you!'

A silent, brusque inclination of his head was all the response he made, and it was only as she sat back again that a new thought struck her.

'But you do realise that you've just talked yourself out of a job?'

She could barely see his face in the gathering shadows, couldn't read anything of his reaction. She only knew that even as she spoke the thought of him not being at the party with her made her feel suddenly terribly lost, totally bereft in a way that had nothing to do with any concern for her father's approval.

'But you still have to come!'

That brought his head round sharply.

'*Have* to?'

The question stabbed at her from the darkness, bringing home just how close she had come to giving herself away.

Giving *what* away? Georgia found she couldn't even answer that herself.

'You can't let me down.' Hastily she tried to cover her tracks. 'You have to come! I *paid* for you.'

It was the wrong thing to say; she knew it from his sudden ominous stillness, the dangerously taut silence.

'And of course you want value for money.' The harshness of his voice when he finally spoke seemed to splinter the atmosphere inside the car. 'But you needn't worry, darling.' Black cynicism turned the endearment into an insult. 'I wasn't about to renege on my promise. I know only too well what I *owe* you.'

'That's—' Georgia began, but he wouldn't let her speak.

'You paid,' he declared almost brutally. 'You paid and I'll deliver.'

'You'll deliver?' she echoed in confusion.

'I'll be there.'

Leaning past her, he wrenched at the handle, pushing the door open with a violence that spoke only too clearly of how anxious he was to be rid of her, how much he wanted to see the back of her.

'I'll be there, darling, just as you wanted,' he snarled, reaching for the dress box from the back seat and shoving it into her hands. 'I'll stand at your side and I'll smile and dance attendance on you. I'll put on the act of my life, give you just what you paid for. And no one—*no one*—will ever guess just how far from the truth the whole bloody farce will be.'

If he had actually physically pushed her from the car he couldn't have made his feelings more plain. By the time Georgia had stumbled inelegantly onto the pavement he had already slammed the door shut again and was pressing his foot on the accelerator with a force that made the engine roar in protest.

'Lucas!' she tried, but either he couldn't or deliberately wouldn't hear her. And, besides, what could she say?

She had got what she wanted, she told herself drearily. She'd got him to agree to come to the party. But she didn't feel at all good about it.

Lucas wouldn't be coming with her because he wanted to, but only because he felt obliged to, because he owed it to her. And it was the knowledge that he felt that sense of obligation that stabbed at her agonisingly as she watched the car speed off down the street with a squeal of tyres.

Her vision was blurred, and she had to blink hard to clear it in order to watch. It was only as the powerful car finally rounded the corner that she realised that what burned at her eyes were hot, bitter tears of loss.

CHAPTER EIGHT

'IF YOU'RE not going to speak to me at all today, then it's going to be a very long journey.'

'Oh, I'm sorry.'

Lucas's tone made it plain that his apology wasn't in the least sincere—quite the opposite, in fact.

'I was under the impression that any display of interest or affection was to be kept strictly to certain hours, not to begin until we reached your parents' house. But if you want more than that, then of course I'm only too ready to oblige. After all, you're the one who's paying. You'll want value—'

'That wasn't what I meant, and you know it!'

The pointed reminder that any affection or even any interest that he might show her would only be carefully assumed, a pretence put on to convince others, stabbed at Georgia so sharply that she had to fight not to wince visibly. She didn't need any emphasis of the fact that Lucas was only here because he felt obliged to fulfil their agreement. She couldn't have been more painfully aware of that from the start.

'But I did hope that we could at least be *polite*. Surely that isn't too much to ask?'

'No,' Lucas agreed slowly. 'But why do your comments make me think of pots and kettles, and the colour black?'

'Oh, all right.' She had to acknowledge that he had a point. 'So I haven't been exactly chatty either.'

And that was something of an understatement. From

the moment that Lucas had arrived at her house, in fact
long before he had even put in an appearance, she had
been so keyed up that she had moved round her home
as restlessly as a cat on hot bricks. And when he *had*
turned up nothing about him had done anything to settle
her uneasy frame of mind.

For a start, she had been completely thrown by the
way he looked. She had grown so accustomed to seeing
Lucas in those elegant, superbly tailored suits that the
sight of him in elderly denim jeans and a lightweight
cotton sweater in a soft shade of blue-grey had thrown
her very much off balance.

It had been like seeing another man in his place, an
identical twin who was so like the man she knew and
yet so very different. The soft texture of the jumper was
in devastating contrast to the hard power of muscle underneath, making her throat tighten unnervingly so that
she'd had to swallow fiercely to relieve the tension before she had even been able to greet him.

And then there had been the car...

'I should have thanked you for this.'

Aiming for lightness, she touched the elegant dashboard gently, but the truth was that she had been struck
dumb by the sight of the car waiting for her. Had Lucas
remembered how she had described the Morgan as her
fantasy car, or was it just a coincidence?

'I thought you didn't use these cars for entertaining.'

'I decided I ought to do something to mark the occasion. After all, it is your father's sixtieth.'

'Of course.'

She should have known, she told herself. After the
way they had parted the last time, she would never have
expected that Lucas would do anything to please her.
The Morgan would delight her father anyway.

'Well, I suppose there's an extra bonus in your choice
of vehicle.' Bitter disappointment made her voice tart.
'And that is that you're keeping strictly to the speed

limit. I'd anticipated some of your grand prix speeds today.'

The deep grey eyes swung to her face for a second, one brow lifting in that familiar questioning gesture.

'Nearly two hundred miles per hour on the motorway? You must be joking. You'd have to—'

'Have to what?' Georgia asked, intrigued by the way he clammed up suddenly, assuming an intent concentration on the road ahead that was quite unnecessary considering the few other cars around.

'It doesn't matter.'

'Yes, it does.'

She was determined not to let him dodge the question, suddenly feeling that she could actually sense the faintest chink in the armour of impenetrable composure with which he surrounded himself.

'You'd have to what?'

Lucas shrugged indifferently.

'To be completely mad. When you've looked death in the face in the shape of a pile of twisted, blazing metal that might have been the last thing you knew on this earth, then you realise there's much more to life than speed—or even winning.'

Of course, she should have realised that he was thinking of the crash that had brought a premature end to his racing career.

'But you were unhurt, and you reacted so—'

'Coolly?' Lucas interjected on a cynical note. 'Never turned a hair? That's what the papers said, isn't it? Do you want to know the real truth, Gia? Would you like to know how I actually felt at the time?'

'Yes.'

The response came without her thinking, ignoring the sardonic note in his voice that was meant actively to discourage any such agreement and surprising even Georgia herself with just how much she did want to know.

'I couldn't believe that I was still alive, that I was actually standing there, watching the car burn. It didn't seem right—or fair.'

'Not fair? But Lucas—'

She couldn't bear to think of it having been otherwise, the thought of that strong, perfect body being torn and mangled sending a sensation like cold, creeping footsteps down her spine.

'My best friend had died in a similar crash only the month before. I walked away, but he perished.'

'I see.'

'Do you?' The words were rough and harsh. 'I wonder if you do; if you really *see*.'

'Oh, I admit that I've never experienced anything like that, or even anything close. But I can imagine.'

And one thing she felt she did understand now was why he was so casual, so careless in his relationships with women. She could well imagine that, having come so close to death, he would want to live life to the full, experience all its pleasures, kiss every beautiful girl he met—more than kiss…

'Can you?' Lucas demanded. 'Can you imagine how it felt to know that I, who had no responsibilities, no dependants, had emerged unscathed while Tony, who had a wife, and a baby on the way—'

Breaking off sharply, he shook his dark head in disquiet.

'And I was the one who had to tell Nessa. I think that was still in my mind during that later race, ruining my concentration. That was when I knew I had to stop racing; it no longer seemed to matter.'

'And Nessa? Do you mean Vanessa—the one we bought the dress from?'

'The same. She was seven months pregnant when Tony was killed, and the shock sent her into premature labour. If she'd lost the baby, her last link with Tony, I don't think she'd have wanted to go on. That's when I first came into contact with the special baby unit.'

'And that's why you were at the auction.'

Lucas nodded soberly. 'They saved Nessa's life, and the baby's. She's my goddaughter, so naturally I'd do anything to help.'

'Even to the extent of travelling all the way to Yorkshire for some party you've no desire at all to go to. I'm sorry.'

'Don't be stupid, Gia. Time spent in the company of a beautiful woman is never wasted.'

Which came so close to confirming her own thoughts about the effect of the crash on him that it had her biting hard on her lower lip in distress.

'And you needn't worry. I'll give you value for money.'

'I told you, the money doesn't matter! I can afford it.'

'Your business must be doing well.'

'It is.' She couldn't disguise her pride in the fact. 'After all, I've been in London for five years now. My first big break was when I did out a house for a friend and her husband. They were newly married and didn't have all that much money, so I did it for peanuts, really, but his sister was Elize Birtwhistle.'

'The actress? The one in the TV soap?'

'The very same. She loved what I'd done with Helena's home, and as she'd just bought herself this huge townhouse—and I *mean* huge—she asked me to decorate it for her. Naturally her friends saw what I'd done, and liked it, and—well, things just snowballed from there.'

'You make it sound simple,' Lucas put in. 'I'm sure it wasn't as easy as that.'

'I was lucky.'

'You had luck, yes, in that you got a good break, but it was your talent that got you noticed. You're very good at what you do.'

'You haven't seen any of my work!'

'I've seen your home. And I have seen one of your commissions, though I wasn't aware of it at the time. You did up a small hotel some friends of mine own.'

'The Stocks? Down by the river? Oh, I enjoyed that! All those crazily shaped rooms. But I wouldn't have thought it was your sort of place.'

'Just because I used to drive around in sleek, ultra-modern cars doesn't necessarily mean that all my tastes are quite so minimalist. I like my home—and hotels—to be much more on the lines of old-fashioned comfort.'

'The Stocks is certainly that,' Gia agreed, her laughter only a little forced in order to hide the fact that once more he had surprised her. But her amusement became more genuine as she turned a swift glance on the powerful length of his back, the arrogant carriage of that dark head. 'Do you go there often?'

'I probably visit Gerry and Pat about once a month. And, yes—' disconcertingly he had picked up on her train of thought as easily as sensitive radar detected the slightest signal '—I do find my height a disadvantage in the bar.'

'All those beams!' Georgia's laughter became more relaxed in response to his wry grin. 'You must spend all your time ducking them.'

'I was black and blue the first time I visited,' Lucas admitted ruefully. 'Of course, it doesn't worry either Gerry or Pat, neither being an inch over five feet six.'

'I suppose that must have been average for most people at the time that The Stocks was actually built.'

The atmosphere in the car had lightened considerably, she was relieved to see, and suddenly the journey ahead seemed to hold out a whole new promise, no longer stretching ahead as a difficult, uncomfortable amount of time to be filled.

'Well, Richard the Lionheart was described as being a giant of a man when he was probably only six foot or so. It was just that he stood out amongst—or rather, *above*—the men of the time.'

'I know the feeling!' Georgia said meaningfully. 'Have you any idea what it's like to be at a party or a dance, to have someone ask you to dance and then watch his face change as you stand up—and up.'

'More fool him. Only a complete simpleton would want to wish away a single one of your glorious inches. I don't really think that a smaller woman could ever be truly elegant in the way that you are.'

Georgia's heart skipped a beat in response to the softly spoken compliment, but just as it threatened to soar in delight she clamped down hard on it, imposing a ruthless sense of reality.

'Very nicely put, Lucas!' She was pleased with the casual lightness of her tone. 'I knew I'd chosen the right man, that I could rely on you. But don't use up all your collection of flattering remarks before we've even arrived.'

'Oh, that wasn't part of what you've paid for,' Lucas assured her with deadly softness. 'That one came for free. And believe me, it was definitely *not* flattery.'

He gave her a second or two to digest this, long enough for the heat to fade from her face and her heart to settle down slightly, then shook her completely by adding, 'And you have no need to worry that I might run out of compliments to pay you. As far as that's concerned, I haven't even started yet.'

Which was guaranteed to freeze her tongue in her mouth and have her staring out of the window in total confusion, her unfocused eyes staring blankly, taking in nothing of the countryside through which they were passing. She heard Lucas's soft laughter and knew that he was well aware of the way she was feeling.

'Oh, Gia, Gia,' he said softly. 'How are we ever going to convince your father if this is the way you react to even the simplest compliment?'

Georgia's breath hissed through her teeth as she straightened her shoulders, turning stiffly towards him with her head held high, hazel eyes blazing defiantly into his dark ones.

'My father isn't going to be convinced by the sort of pretence he can see through at a glance! And, if I'm honest, I've gone off the whole idea of that plan altogether.'

'Really? And just what do you intend to put in its place?'

'Nothing. I've decided you were right in what you said. If he can't take me as I am, then I'm not going to try and change or play up to his idea of what a daughter should be.'

'I see. And just where do I fit in to all this? Precisely what do you want from me?'

'Nothing.'

Her voice was less certain this time, his question sparking off all sorts of reactions inside her head and heart, responses she would have found difficult to explain even to herself. What she truly *wanted* was not something she dared put into words.

'I mean, let's just go back to the original arrangement.'

'Which is?'

'You know! I'm going to a party and I need an escort. You're that man—end of story.'

'And that's it?'

'That's it.' Georgia nodded decisively, more decisively than she actually felt. 'So now I've made it easy for you. You no longer have to think up impossible compliments or pretend to a passion you don't actually feel.'

'I don't?' There was a strange note in Lucas's voice. 'I don't,' he repeated with a very different intonation. 'Pity—I was really quite looking forward to all that.'

'Well, now you can stop looking forward to it.' And, privately, she took the liberty of doubting very much that he had ever done so. 'Because it's not going to happen. All I want from you is that you act as my—my partner.'

'Strictly business,' Lucas murmured.

'That's right. No show, no pretence…'

'No compliments?'

That stopped her dead, her composure rocked by the way he had sounded almost regretful. She wouldn't be human if she didn't admit to something close to an aching sense of loss at the thought of hearing no more of those sensually spoken compliments, the carefully phrased words of praise that, even though they were deliberately calculated, would turn any woman's head.

'Well…' She was afraid that her voice betrayed her and tried to make it firmer. 'From now on I would prefer it if you stuck to being strictly honest. I want no outrageous flattery, certainly.'

'No flattery,' Lucas agreed with uncomplimentary speed. 'From now on, I'll say only what I really feel.'

It was what she had asked for, Georgia told herself, forcing her attention back to the passing scenery. It was what she'd told herself she wanted. So why did she suddenly feel that unknowingly she'd handed him a two-edged sword, a weapon on which both sides of the blade gleamed brilliantly, wickedly sharp?

That thought resurfaced with a new and unnerving force when, having left the motorway behind them and travelled through many winding country roads, she gave the final directions needed to reach their destination.

'Turn right here, then first left. Up this drive.'

As they came to a halt she fully expected some comment about the size and imposing substance of the house. At the very least, she had thought there might be a reference to the way its grey Yorkshire stone looked as hard and uncompromising as the residents of that county had the reputation of being. But Lucas simply switched off the engine without a word and stretched lazily, easing muscles cramped from so long in the same position.

'So here we are,' he said at last. 'Will anyone be at home?'

'Oh, they'll all be there,' Georgia assured him. 'Certainly Mum and Dad will, and, if I know anything, my sisters will too.'

Her mother would have wasted no time in letting everyone know that Georgia was bringing 'someone special' to the party, and she knew that her family would not be able to contain their curiosity until the evening.

Drawing a deep breath, she got out of the car and turned towards the house.

'Come on, then, let's get this over with.'

Not waiting for him to join her, she marched towards the huge old oak door, determined resolution carrying her as far as the top of the wide stone steps before abruptly deserting her. It was one thing to declare that her father had to accept her as she was, quite another to know that she had to face the man who had always made her feel such a disappointment.

'Gia—wait…'

Lucas's voice was surprisingly soft. As she turned slowly to face him she saw that with his dark eyes narrowed against the sun he was watching her closely, studying her face as if he could actually see into her head and read her thoughts.

'Come here.'

His arms came round her, holding her close. His dark head lowered and he kissed her with such thoroughness, such sensual expertise that if she hadn't had the support of his strength she felt that her knees might have buckled, giving way and depositing her unceremoniously on the top step.

Her mind was reeling, heat flooding every nerve, and she was unable to hold back the instinctive, powerful response that her body demanded. Within the space of a heartbeat she was kissing him too, without a thought for where she was or who might see them.

When at last Lucas released her, her breathing was raw and uneven, her scalp tingled where his hands had twisted in her hair and she knew that her cheeks burned with fiery colour underneath over-bright hazel eyes.

'What—what was that for?' she managed, her voice cracking on the words.

'Encouragement,' Lucas told her smilingly. 'Because you looked like Daniel about to enter the lions' den. And because I wanted to.' The smile grew wider. 'And so that now you actually look the part.'

'Part?' Georgia asked in confusion, having no idea what he meant.

'Now you look like a woman who has a man hopelessly in love with her.'

In her bemused and bewildered state of mind, it took Georgia a couple of seconds to register exactly what he had said, and several more to remember that she had told him that this particular pretence was no longer necessary, that she couldn't go through with it. But before she could say anything to remind him of that fact she heard footsteps in the hall, and as the door was pulled open the moment was lost.

CHAPTER NINE

GEORGIA sat in front of her dressing table in the bedroom that had been hers as a child, her elbows on the polished surface, chin cupped in the palms of her hands as she stared into her own face reflected in the mirror. For the past half an hour or so she had been trying to reach some understanding of the way things had developed since they had arrived at her parents' house.

'How could it have happened?' she asked herself out loud, looking into eyes that a stunned sense of shock had turned a dark, mossy green. The way that her sense of mental balance had been so badly rocked showed in a new tension that drew her skin tight across her cheekbones. 'How could things have changed so suddenly?'

But, of course, it hadn't really been sudden. It had crept up on her like some thief in the night, coming up behind her with a club or other, similar weapon. At least, that was what it had felt like when it had all exploded in her mind with the force of a blow to the back of her head.

From the moment that the door had opened to reveal her mother's smiling face with, as she had expected, both her older sisters hovering in the background, she hadn't had any time to think further about the way that Lucas had reacted outside. She had been swept into all the excitement of the prodigal's return home, exchanging hugs and greetings and introducing Lucas to the female members of her family, whose reactions had been everything she had expected.

Both Liz and Meg had been clearly stunned to find their ugly duckling sister in the company of such an undeniable hunk. Their fluttering eyelashes and rather breathless voices had been a clear indication that, married or not, they were far from immune to Lucas's own particularly lethal brand of masculine appeal.

And, of course, he had set himself to charm them as only he could. Switching on that stunning smile, he had treated all three women to the sort of concentrated attention that, as Georgia already knew to her cost, did devastating things to any susceptible female heart.

She had watched her mother and sisters melt under its laser-like impact, and within five minutes of their arrival had known that, like Julius Caesar, Lucas could claim that he had come, seen and conquered.

So far so good, but of course she had always known that they would prove to be no problem. Her father was something else, and she had been fully expecting the autocratic tones that had reached them in the first lull in the excited chatter.

'For God's sake, are you women going to stay out there in that hall gossiping all afternoon? Why don't you get yourselves in here so I can see you?'

That was her father all over, Georgia reflected ruefully. He would never come to them; they had to go to him.

It was just as she had expected. He was sitting in his usual place, in the high-backed leather chair that stood closest to the fire, dominating the room, and he made no move to get to his feet as she crossed the thick carpet to greet him.

'Hello, Dad. Happy birthday! You're looking well.'

In fact he looked little different, as he always did, in spite of the length of time since she had last seen him. Perhaps his hair had a little more grey in it, and the lines around his clear green eyes were rather more obvious, but he was still as he had always been: a powerful, bull-

like man with a thick neck and broad chest, his head
held proudly erect.

'Of course I'm well! I'm sixty, not ninety! Plenty of
life in me yet!'

He turned his face to receive her kiss, but even as she
pressed her lips to his cheek she knew that he was already looking past her. His gaze had gone over her head
to the man who had come into the room behind her and
was now standing waiting, dark eyes alert and watchful,
until she was ready to introduce him.

And that was when it had happened. Georgia sighed
and made to push a disturbed hand through her hair, only
stopping herself just in time before she ruined the elegant coil into which she had arranged it ready for the
party that evening.

'Well, now, who's this?' her father had said, and she
had turned, holding out a hand to Lucas, to draw him
closer.

'Dad, I'd like you to meet Lucas Mallory.'

She had looked straight into her father's face as she'd
spoken and knew exactly the moment that he had registered just who the other man was. She'd seen his expression change, the interest quickening in his eyes, and
it had been everything she would have said that she had
dreamed of ever since she had come up with this scheme
in the first place.

'And that's the trouble!' she sighed aloud, shaking her
head at the memory.

Because it *had* been just what she had hoped for: the
look on her father's face, the expression of admiration
mixed with disbelief. She had known that she had
stunned him, amazed and impressed him, and yet it had
meant nothing at all.

For an apocalyptic moment she had frozen, numb with
shock and confusion, not knowing why she should feel
this way, why her father's reaction should mean so little.

But then Lucas had stepped forward, his hand out-stretched.

'Delighted to meet you, Mr Harding.'

Just a few simple words, but when she'd heard them the scene had seemed to shift, dissolve and reform, her heart turning over in her chest. Her eyes had flown to Lucas's face and the full impact of just what had happened had hit home with a force that made her reel.

Somewhere along the line—almost, it seemed, in the time between that kiss at the door and the moment that she had introduced Lucas to her father—she had finally lost her grip on the situation altogether. The reins she had thought she held securely once more had been snatched from her hands, and the runaway horse of her feelings was out of her control once and for all.

Because the problem was that the words 'strictly business' no longer applied in any way to what was happening. It was all feeling, and nothing else mattered now that she knew. She had fallen in love with Lucas Mallory, giving him her heart without even knowing that she had lost it, and all the wishing and thinking in the world wouldn't bring it back.

'So, what do I do now?' she asked her reflection, jumping nervously as a sudden rap came at her door, as if in answer to her question.

'Gia?' Lucas's voice carried clearly across the room. 'Are you in there?'

She was strongly tempted to stay silent and pretend the room was empty. Lucas was the last person she wanted to see while her thoughts and feelings were in such a tangle, and she felt unable to assume any sort of mask to hide her vulnerability from those probing dark eyes. It was either that or tell him to go to hell and leave her alone.

She had had enough trouble getting through the afternoon. The hours that had passed since the moment of revelation had seemed to tick away so slowly. She had been forced to spend her time making polite conversation, smiling with a false air of relaxed carelessness, when deep inside she was a bundle of twisted nerves and anxious concern. All afternoon she had been longing to get away by herself to take a long, calm look at what had happened and try to decide just what she was going to do.

'*Gia!*' Lucas's tone had sharpened.

It was no good. Tossing down the mascara that she had been using to enhance her long lashes, Georgia squared her shoulders and marched to the door, yanking it open with a force that betrayed her inner tension.

'Yes?' Her voice was too high and tight, hiding her unease behind a snappishly bad-tempered front. 'What do you want?'

If only he didn't look so wonderful, she might find it easier to cope, she told herself despairingly. But there was little hope of that. In the severe formality of evening dress, Lucas was once more the charismatic 'star attraction' of the charity auction, sleek and dark and devastating as a jungle cat.

But now the devastating impact of his naturally lethal attraction was heightened and intensified by the force of her feelings for him. And those feelings were so strong that even if he had disguised himself, hidden those stunning features behind a mask, clothed that imposing body in rags, she would still have known it was him.

'And good evening to you too.' Lucas's response was swift and sardonic, searing over nerves already stretched to breaking point with the effort of concealing the emotions she felt must burn in her eyes or be stamped onto her forehead in letters of fire. 'Is this how you usually greet someone who's come to check that you're all right?'

'Oh, I'm sorry!'

Georgia caught herself up hastily. If she wasn't careful she would give herself away, make him suspect... A shiver of apprehension feathered down her spine at the thought.

'It's just I'm a little on edge.'

'That seems to be the understatement of the year,' Lucas returned, startling her into a gasp of shock as he took hold of her arms, moving her backwards into the room and kicking the door shut behind him.

'Lucas, no! My mother—'

One dark eyebrow quirked upwards swiftly, questioning her words.

'The oh, so old-fashioned Mrs Harding?' he drawled satirically. 'The lady who you claimed would have a fit at the thought of any sort of impropriety, such as the two of us being alone together in a bedroom of all places? Are we talking about the same lady—the one who just sent me upstairs to fetch you?'

'Mum did?'

'Not to mention the encouraging comments and smiles from the two elder daughters of the house.'

Now, that she *could* believe. Meg and Liz had already taken every possible opportunity to quiz her about Lucas's presence in her life, taking her aside to pester her with questions. She had been hard put to it to find answers for them, not least because her mind had been only half on what they were saying.

'And of course your father...'

'*Dad!*'

Georgia turned a frankly sceptical look on Lucas, only to see from his wicked smile in response that he had meant what he said.

'He seemed to be of the opinion that I was the only person who could "talk some sense into that girl".'

He slid into a mimicry of her father's gruff tones that had her admitting admiration for its wicked accuracy.

'I was to tell you to stop mooning about up here and to get downstairs and join the party.'

'Oh, God!'

The realisation that her father seemed to have swallowed the fiction of her relationship with Lucas even more completely than she had ever anticipated gave another, unbearable twist to Georgia's already hypersensitive nerves.

'Why so devastated, darling? After all, that's what you wanted, isn't it? You should be happy that your plan has worked out perfectly—hasn't it?'

When Georgia could only nod silently, unable to form any more coherent response, he frowned suddenly, moving swiftly to place a strong hand under her chin and lift her face towards his.

'Or is there something else; something you haven't told me?'

Only that I love you, and that I don't know how I'm going to get through tonight without letting that slip, she thought. Because, if she did let any such emotion show, then Lucas, who had made it plain that he had only come with her today in order to fulfil the obligation he felt towards the premature baby unit, would probably just turn and walk away, going out of her life for ever, without even a single look back.

That would have been hard enough to cope with before, but now, when everyone in her family seemed to have accepted them as a couple, it was going to be almost impossible to handle.

'Of course not!' She forced herself to answer him. 'It's just…'

'Just…?' Lucas prompted hardly, when her voice failed her. Dark eyes searched her face, making her stomach quail at the thought of what he might read there. 'Ah, I see. He's only a man, Gia, just another human being.'

So he thought she was still fearful of her father's reaction, Georgia reflected on a twist of distress. Perhaps it was better to let him believe that that was what *was* behind her unease, though she admitted to a bitter sense

of irony at the thought that never before in her life had
Ben Harding's opinion actually mattered less.

'Come on, Gia.' Lucas's voice seemed to curl around
her tautly strung nerves, tightening the knots in them.
'You can handle it. But maybe these will help.'

From his pocket he pulled out a small jeweller's box,
pushing it into her unresisting hand, smiling at her gasp
of delight as she opened it.

'I was sure that you'd wear your hair up tonight, so I
hoped they'd do.'

'They'll more than do! Lucas, they're perfect!'

As much to ease her inner tension as in any sort of
vanity, Georgia spun away from him to pin the golden
drops in her ears, turning back again with a brilliant
smile.

'Well?'

'Almost as lovely as the lady I bought them for,' he
murmured, a new huskiness in his voice, and the sudden
darkness of his eyes sent her heart into a jerky dance
that made breathing difficult. 'Come here—'

She couldn't resist the soft-voiced command, though
she knew what was coming, and she went into his arms
with her mouth already raised for a kiss that was warm
and slow and infinitely sweet. She was drowning, very
definitely going down for the third time, with no hope
of salvation...

'Mallory!'

Her father's bellow made it sound almost as if he was
standing just outside the door instead of downstairs in
the hall.

'Are you planning on staying up there all night?'

'Coming!'

Lucas smiled deep into Georgia's eyes, his expression
touched with a hint of conspiracy that lifted her spirits.

'Ready?' he asked lightly, and she lifted her chin determinedly.

'Ready,' she told him firmly, but all her new-found

confidence almost deserted her when he brushed one last featherlight kiss across the tip of her nose before tucking her arm under his.

'That's my girl. Come on, let's show them!'

My girl—my girl. The words reverberated inside Georgia's head as she made her way downstairs. With Lucas at her side, she knew she could handle anything, cope with whatever the evening threw at her. But she knew that his presence here tonight was for appearance only. Tomorrow morning…

But, no, she wouldn't think of that! For tonight at least, she *was* Lucas's girl, and, like Cinderella, she had at least until the clock struck twelve to enjoy the magic of the evening. She wouldn't let any thought of tomorrow intrude, would allow no trace of 'if only' to spoil things.

Tonight was hers. She was wearing a spectacular dress, had these beautiful earrings and the man she loved at her side. She would drink champagnes, dance with Lucas and be happy for a few hours at least—and tomorrow could take care of itself.

To her amazement, it worked. From the moment that they made their way downstairs, her hand on Lucas's arm, she felt as if she was floating on air, her feet never touching the ground.

She moved through the evening in a brilliant golden bubble that enclosed her perfectly, repelling all doubts or worries while at the same time surrounding her with a feeling of warmth and pure joy so that time passed in a heady blur. She knew that she talked, greeting old friends and making new acquaintances, that she sipped champagne and even ate a little, though she couldn't remember what—the only thing she was really aware of was the man she loved.

Lucas rarely moved from her side, and even if he did she had only to look up to find that their eyes met immediately, no matter where he was in the room. His arms were round her when they danced, and the intoxicating cocktail of scent that was created by the combination of his cologne and the clean, warm smell of his body went straight to her head like some potent drug when he held her close.

She felt that she was breathing in his presence, absorbing it through every sense, every pore in her skin. Even on the rare occasions when they were separated she could still feel him, her own personal radar seeking him out as irresistibly as a compass needle must always be drawn to the north.

And so she found it something of a shock to realise that several hours had passed, that the party was just about over and their guests were departing in a flurry of hugs and kisses, leaving the big house suddenly silent and empty. The evening had been surprisingly warm for early May, and now the atmosphere was disturbingly close and oppressive, the threat of thunder heavy in the air.

Her sisters and their families had left for their own homes, and, worn out with the excitement and all the organising, her mother had taken herself off to bed. Lucas had disappeared somewhere, and, not wanting to go without saying goodnight to him, Georgia wandered through the deserted house, stopping dead in shock when she found her father lingering in the conservatory.

'Hello, Dad!' she said in some surprise. 'I thought you'd be off to bed by now.'

'Just having a nightcap before I go.' Ben lifted a half-empty brandy glass.

'It's been a good night, hasn't it? Have you enjoyed yourself?'

'I have that. And I'll tell you something, it's been good to see you in this house again—especially with that man of yours at your side.'

'You like Lucas, then?'

Georgia refused to let the fact that it was Lucas's presence that had delighted her father hurt her. It was only what she had expected after all.

The grey head nodded firmly.

'You've got yourself a good man there, lass, a real man—not like those no-goods you used to hang around with. If you're wise, you'll hang onto him and not let him slip away because of some silly concern with your job.'

'I do have a business to think of, Dad!'

Her father dismissed her protest with an imperious wave of his hand.

'You shouldn't be bothering with business! That's not a woman's concern; it's men's work. Women should be at home, taking care of their husbands, with a couple of kiddies in the nursery by your age. You've no reason to bother with a career.'

He made the word sound like the worst possible sort of offence, and Georgia fought down the familiar prickle of irritation. They had had this argument countless times before, and, try as she might, she had never, ever managed to change his way of thinking.

But this time she couldn't muster any argument to counter his because his mention of children had suddenly resounded in her mind with all the force of a nuclear explosion. Just the idea of it left her incapable of forming any thoughts beyond secret, impossible images of the children Lucas might father—tall and dark like himself, with wide grey eyes.

'Not that any of the men you knew before were worth having.' Her father hadn't noticed her abstracted state. 'But this one—*this* one's different. He's a man you could be proud to claim as a husband.'

'Dad!' Georgia began despairingly, but everything she had been about to say evaporated from her thoughts like mist before the sun in the moment when another voice took up the conversation from behind her, bringing her spinning round in shock.

'On the contrary.' Lucas spoke from the doorway, his dark eyes flicking only briefly over Georgia's face before fixing on her father, all his attention concentrated on the older man. 'I really think that the opposite is more like the truth, Mr Harding.'

'What are you talking about?' Georgia's father frowned. 'I don't see what you mean.'

'I think you do,' Lucas told him coolly. 'Or if you don't you're not the man I took you to be. Your daughter has no need of any man to bolster her standing in anyone's eyes. She's beautiful, intelligent, strong and resourceful, and above all independent. And as such she's a woman I would be proud to have as my wife.'

Georgia knew that her mouth had fallen open in stunned amazement, and she closed it hastily with a distinct snap. Had Lucas had some sort of a brainstorm? This was most definitely not what she had had in mind when she had asked him to accompany her here. It was way over and above the demands of their arrangement— with a vengeance!

'Lucas—' she began hesitantly, but he ignored her completely.

'And I would expect that any man with the smallest degree of intelligence would be delighted to have a daughter like yours. You must be very proud of all she's done—setting up her own business in that way, and so far from home, asking for no help or support from you. She's earned a tremendous reputation over the past few years—deservedly so, don't you agree?'

He had Ben Harding cornered, and the faintest curl of amusement at the corner of his mouth told Georgia that he knew it.

She herself had to struggle with a set of distinctly ambiguous feelings. The stab of distress at her father's stubborn refusal to acknowledge her success warred with a slightly nervous desire to giggle at the expression on his face, in which the desire to please his impressive guest struggled with long-ingrained prejudice.

'Oh, well, yes. She's got a good head on her shoulders, I'll grant you that,' he admitted gruffly.

It was more than she had ever had from him in the past, but just as she acknowledged the faint glow of pleasure it brought Ben Harding spoke again.

'Mind you, I just wish she'd settle down and give some thought to providing me with a couple more grandsons.' He drained his glass and got to his feet, yawning slightly. 'And now, if you'll excuse me, I'll head for my bed. It's been a long day, and we have an early start planned for the morning if your offer of giving me a chance to drive that car of yours still holds.'

'Of course—say eight o'clock, before we set off back to London.'

When the older man had left the room, and moving well out of his earshot, Lucas turned to Georgia, a wry smile on his wide mouth.

'Stubborn old so and so! I've never met anyone so recalcitrant!'

'I did warn you.' Georgia's laughter was uneven. 'But it doesn't matter,' she added, surprising herself by finding that she spoke nothing but the truth.

It *didn't* matter, didn't hurt any more. All that was important to her was Lucas himself, though she knew that she didn't dare to connect the things he had said tonight to the promise he had made in the car just before they had first arrived.

'I'll say only what I really feel,' he had told her, but she didn't allow herself to think that it could be true of the declaration he had made to her father. That had only been meant to drive his point home, she was sure.

'He left rather quickly. Was it something I said?'

'If you want to know the truth,' Georgia told him, knowing only too well the way that her father's mind worked, 'I think he believes that if he left us alone then you might actually propose to me.'

And just for a second she was weak enough to dream of it too. If Lucas were to ask her to be his wife, then there was no doubt in her mind that the struggle to win her father's approval would be over once and for all.

But almost immediately she dismissed the idea. That was not how she wanted it to be, and besides, the silence that had greeted her impetuous remark had now stretched out so long, becoming so brittle, that she felt that the thud of her heart was loud enough to shatter it into tiny pieces. Lucas's stillness was suddenly so total as to be worrying.

'Or perhaps,' he said at last, without a trace of a smile, 'that we might do something about creating those damn grandsons he's so set on.'

'Hardly!'

That thought was so disturbing that a burning heat flooded through her, making her feel as if she was in the grip of a raging fever, with a temperature that threatened to make her delirious. She had to be crazy in some way, because, just for a second, she could have sworn that Lucas was actually serious.

'I told you, my parents are very old-fashioned.'

She wouldn't have been able to find words to describe the look that he gave her, only knew that it added to the unnerving, unsettled feeling that was like sharp pins and needles all over her body. It was very late, and yet she had never felt less like going to bed. Sleep would be impossible, she knew, unless she did something to work off this appalling restlessness—and besides, she couldn't stay here with Lucas and not give in to the urge to touch him—do more than touch.

'I fancy a walk!' she announced abruptly, knowing she had startled him by the way his head went back sharply.

'At this time of the night?'

'Time doesn't matter. Besides, there's a full moon out.'

'There's also a storm brewing.'

'All the more reason to get some air while we can. And the possibility of thunder means it's incredibly mild. So, are you coming?'

In the few seconds it took him to consider his answer she suddenly knew with a shocking clarity just how much she wanted him with her, so much so that she felt her heart might actually break if he didn't agree. But at last he nodded his dark head slowly.

'But you're hardly dressed for a hike.'

'And neither are you! But it won't be a *hike*, just a stroll round the grounds, and we usually keep flat shoes by the back door.'

Leading him into the hall, she proved her point by exchanging her dainty gold sandals for a pair of comfortable black slip-on loafers, ignoring how incongruous they looked with the cream dress. Reaching up, she took her cashmere wrap from the hooks above.

'And this will protect me from any chills.'

The moonlit gardens were every bit as beautiful as she had expected, each bush and shrub bathed in pale, silvery rays that turned them into a spectacular fairyland. It was a magical world in which reality was suspended, one in which it felt perfectly right and natural to slip her hand under Lucas's arm and move closer to the warm strength of his powerful body.

For some minutes they walked in companionable silence, their steps matching perfectly. Georgia's heart was singing a soaring song of contentment, and she knew she would be happy to continue like this for ever. But then, rounding a corner in the path, Lucas came to a sudden halt.

'What's that over there?' A wave of his hand indicated the small, octagonal-shaped building at the far end of the lawn.

'Oh, that's the old summerhouse. It was my hide-out when I was a kid, but I haven't been inside it for years.'

As she spoke a lightning flash illuminated their path, making it almost as bright as day. It was followed very quickly by a crash of thunder that made it plain that the storm which had threatened was now upon them, breaking directly overhead.

'It looks like we'll have to take shelter there now!' she gasped, breaking into a run as the heavens opened and the rain poured down, soaking through her wrap in seconds. 'Come on!'

Lucas was right behind her as she reached the summerhouse.

'The key should be— Oh, yes, here it is!'

A moment later the door swung open and, laughing in excitement, shaking the raindrops from her face, she stumbled inside. The light from the moon shone clearly in the interior of the small building, and suddenly all her memories flooded back, stilling her face as she turned round slowly, lost in recollection.

'It's just as I remember it. Lucas—'

He was standing still on the threshold, his eyes deep and darkly inscrutable, his expression unreadable. Seeing him like that made her heart jerk uncomfortably, though she was unable to say whether in delight or fear.

'Come inside and shut the door!'

She hid her uncertainty behind lightness, catching hold of his hands and drawing him further into the dusty-floored room.

'We'll be quite comfortable; there's an old daybed here.'

Still holding his hands, she pulled him across to it, pushing aside the plastic protective covering and sinking down onto the cotton-covered mattress, tugging Lucas down beside her while outside the thunder crashed again and the rain pounded against the wooden roof.

'I used to bring my books out here and study for my exams.'

She knew she was chattering just to counteract his silence, needing to fill it with something, anything, before it began to prey on her nerves.

'And sometimes Meg and Liz and I would sneak out here at night, just like this, and we'd cuddle up together and scare each other silly with ghost stories, tales of ghouls and goblins, and things that go bump…'

Lucas's silence had a disturbing, watchful quality about it, stilling her tongue and bringing wide, wary eyes to his strongly carved face that was thrown into eerie shadows by the moonlight. Georgia wondered just what he was thinking behind that impenetrable mask, unable to gain any clues from his shuttered expression.

'…in the night,' she finished, her voice losing all power.

'Do you know how beautiful you are?' Lucas obviously hadn't been listening to a word she said. 'In this unearthly light you look positively ethereal—otherworldly.'

'You're flattering me again. I told you not…' Her voice failed completely as Lucas shook his head in adamant rejection of her protest.

'Not flattery, Gia. Remember, I told you I would only say the things that I really meant. So when I tell you that you are the most beautiful woman I have ever seen you can believe I mean every word I say. Because that is what you are. There's just no competition. You see, you were wrong about your sisters.'

He shook his head with a wry smile at her protesting murmur.

'Oh, they're pretty enough in their own way. But they're like dolls, stereotypes of what ''attractive'' women should be, while you—you're a glorious, strong, elegant woman from the top of your shining head…' his mouth kissed away a raindrop from her forehead '...to the soles of your slender feet.'

'I...' But she could manage no more. Twice her mouth opened, only to close again without making a sound.

'And now that all you told me, all the rules you imposed that put this whole damned situation onto a strictly business footing no longer apply—'

Seeing her puzzled frown, he laughed, the sound low and sensual in the silence before the next roar of thunder.

'Twenty-four hours, Gia—that was the arrangement. Midnight to midnight. But midnight has long gone, my lovely Cinderella. It's another day now.'

He slid along the daybed towards her, eyes black as pitch, and as another flash of lightning lit the sky Georgia shivered, seeing the way it illuminated the unyielding set of his face, leaving her in no doubt as to just what he had in mind.

'Midnight has gone, and with it all the rules you were so determined to impose on me and on yourself. I've fulfilled my part of the bargain, but for a new day we have a new set of rules. My rules, Gia. This time *I'm* setting the terms.'

And as his dark head lowered, his mouth coming down hard on hers, the thunder raging in the sky above them echoed the tempestuous pounding of Georgia's racing heart.

CHAPTER TEN

'ARE you cold?'

Lucas had sensed the involuntary shiver that had run through her body in response to the pressure of his lips, but had interpreted it in the wrong way.

'No, not at all. This place is quite dry and snug. I remember we always kept a couple of blankets in that chest in the corner; they're probably still there.'

It was only when she heard the words spoken out loud that she realised that they sounded not just appeasing but frankly in total agreement with everything his declaration had implied.

And why not? she asked herself in the privacy of her thoughts. Wasn't what Lucas wanted what she wanted too? Hadn't she already abandoned all pretence of keeping the relationship on those strictly confined business lines that she had first aimed for?

And had she really ever believed that he would simply fulfil the terms of their agreement and then go on his way? Had she ever really wanted that? Well, if she ever had, then she certainly no longer felt that way any more.

'We won't need any blankets.' Lucas's voice was gruff, noticeably rougher than before. 'I'll keep you warm.'

And, as if to prove his point, he caught hold of her again, pulling her close and pressing her back against the green cotton of the mattress. As he covered her body with his, his weight holding her prisoner, his mouth took her senses by storm, his kisses fierce and cajoling all in the same moment.

Georgia's hands came up to fasten in the dark silk of his hair, bringing his head down even closer to hers, her lips parting under his to allow the more intimate access he demanded. She couldn't deny him anything, responding instinctively to the yearning, aching sensation that had started up low down in her body.

His hands were on the smooth skin at the nape of her neck, tracing the delicate line of her spine. As she writhed in sensuous response they slid lower, taking with them the zip that fastened her dress, slipping the lacy covering from her shoulders and arms and down, until the cream sheath lay in a discarded pool on the floor.

'Oh, God, Gia...'

Lucas's voice was raw with the same need that was uncoiling inside her, sending tiny electrical impulses along every nerve, awakening every sense to the sight, the sound, the scent of him. He was so close, and yet not close enough.

'This will have to go.'

She couldn't believe it was her own voice, amazed herself with her audacity as she tugged at the lapels of his black dinner jacket. A smile of satisfaction curled her mouth as he moved to help her, shrugging himself out of the elegant garment, tossing it carelessly after her dress as he turned his attention back to her.

'And this...'

Already her fingers were busy with the buttons on his shirt, and it was only when that too joined the growing bundle on the floor that she sighed her contentment. At last her hands were free to wander over the strong lines of his body, curling in sensual delight over the hard power of muscle sheathed by the warm satin of his skin.

Time no longer seemed to be measured in minutes, but in the touch of hands and lips. Each caress, each kiss was illuminated by the flare of lightning alternating with the silver glow of the moon in a spectacular display. And the force of the weather conditions was mirrored in Georgia's own heart. It was as if the storm still raging outside had taken possession of her emotions too as her body trembled beneath his, unable to bear the wanting any longer.

She could have no doubt that Lucas too was in the grip of a matching passion. The kisses he pressed down the slender line of her throat had a fierce, greedy quality about them, as if he wanted to snatch as much as he could from this moment, absorb her into himself, make her completely his.

But when his mouth moved lower, to the soft curves of her breasts, his actions slowed, becoming gentle and sensually indulgent. He drew out each caress, each touch of pleasure, to the point where it was almost unendurable, and above the growl of the thunder Georgia heard her own voice cry out in impatient protest.

'Lucas, please! I can't take any more!'

His only response was the sound of laughter, deep in his throat, before he continued the erotic torture.

Those tormenting lips were moving to one aching nipple, drawing it into the warm cavern of his mouth with agonising slowness. Georgia shivered helplessly, every part of her being seeming to centre on that one tiny point. She was aware of nothing beyond the burning darts of pleasure that radiated outwards from it, flooding every inch of her body and concentrating in a heated ache of need at the centre of her being.

'Lucas...' But now his name was a sigh of encouragement, all protest driven from her mind.

In response, the pressure of his mouth at her breast grew deeper, more urgent, making her writhe frenziedly, her body arching, her hands clenching over his powerful shoulders, nails digging into his skin. She had never felt so driven, so out of control, so desperate. She only knew that if she didn't experience the full satisfaction of his lovemaking she would surely die.

'Die?'

Dimly she heard Lucas's voice, thickened with the same need that burned inside her. The way it was touched with slightly shaken laughter told her that, pushed beyond thought or any degree of control, she had actually spoken the words out loud.

'Oh, no, my lovely Gia, this is what life is all about. It's what we were born for, you and I, how it was always meant to be.'

And he was right, Georgia knew, abandoning herself to the storm they had created between them—wilder, fiercer, more powerful than any of nature's dramatics in the world outside. This was something that could not be stopped, something that was predestined, fated, as old as time and yet as new as the first light of early dawn. She almost felt as if she had been born again, as if before this moment she had never really lived.

'Lucas—' Her voice shook, his name a raw sound on her lips. 'I want you—now—please—'

'Now,' he echoed, kissing the words from her mouth. 'Yes, Gia, now...'

And with one powerful movement he took possession of her completely, his wild cry of triumph blending with the elemental roar of the thunder outside.

Georgia felt as if the storm had invaded their private haven, even the lightning flashes that illuminated the scene seeming like the force of electricity they had created between them. Nature's brilliance flared like the passion that drove them on, throwing Lucas's powerful body into harsh relief against the darkness.

This was what she had feared, this total lack of control, this burning up with sensation. What she had feared and yet what she had wanted from the first. This need obliterated all reason, anything beyond the intensity of pleasure.

The driving rhythm that pounded through her body grew wilder, fiercer, her small cries of pleasure urging Lucas on. Her arms held him close, hands clenching over the strength of his shoulders, her nails digging into his skin.

It was like being on fire, every inch of her body aflame. She was arching, twisting; desire was building like the furnace of a volcano. She was being taken higher, higher, until at last the final explosion took her over the edge and into the oblivion of ecstasy.

It was a long, long time before any sense of reality returned. Georgia's mind and body were so devastated by sensation that she couldn't gather together the shattered remnants of thought or even an understanding of where she was.

It was only when Lucas got up, moving softly on bare feet to the chest she had shown him earlier, that she stirred languidly. With her eyes still closed she registered the silence all around them, stunning, almost unbearable after the wild sounds of only moments before.

'The storm is over,' she murmured dreamily, and heard Lucas's soft laughter as he draped the blanket over her, lying down beside her and pulling her close.

'We drove it away,' he whispered, his breath warm on her cheek. 'Let's face it, it paled in comparison to what there was between you and I.'

'Not enough room in the world for it and us,' Georgia agreed, exhaustion overpowering her.

She was already drifting away on warm waves of sleep, and soon oblivion claimed her, keeping her huddled up in the blankets. She didn't wake until Lucas, more aware of reality than she was capable of being, whispered in her ear.

'Gia, sweetheart, I hate to disturb you when you look so peaceful, but it's almost six. The sun's coming up.'

Slowly and reluctantly Georgia opened her eyes, seeing the change in the light that filled the summerhouse.

Outside she could hear the sounds of the birds' dawn chorus starting up.

'So?'

She didn't want to move. Her whole body ached with the languorous aftermath of passion, every part of her so limp that even her bones felt soft.

'We have to get back to the house. People…'

'No one will be up at such an ungodly hour, not after that late night.'

'Your father will,' Lucas reminded her. 'He and I have an appointment, remember.'

'The car!' Georgia recalled with a groan. And if she knew her father he would be out of bed and ready well before the appointed time, champing at the bit to get his hands on the Morgan's steering wheel.

'Come on, Gia.'

'Oh, all right!'

Forcing herself into action, she lifted her head and stared around her with bleary eyes. She made an effort to move from the daybed, then gave up and subsided back onto the cushions with a groan.

'I can't.'

Lucas's laugh was low and warm. 'Come on, lazy-bones.'

'I can't move!' Georgia protested. 'I'm worn out.'

Focusing her eyes on him at last, she saw that he was already almost fully dressed in the white shirt and black trousers of the suit he had worn to the party. He looked nearly as elegant as he had done the night before.

It was impossible that he should look that way, Georgia reflected. Impossible when she considered the haste with which those clothes had been discarded, the carelessness with which they had been dropped onto the floor, like her own dress.

That thought had her looking round for her own clothes, finding them in a neatly folded bundle by her feet on the bed.

'I can't walk anywhere!'

'Then I'll just have to carry you.'

And, before she could protest, he had dropped the clothes onto her lap before gathering her up, blanket and all, into his strong arms. Kicking open the door, he carried her out into the cool light of the early dawn.

The grass sparkled with the dew on it, and everything had that washed-clean look that came with the peace after a storm. As Georgia peered out from her blanket cocoon she saw that the sky on the horizon was shaded with a wash of pink, bringing to her mind an old rhyme learned years before in her childhood.

Red sky at night, shepherd's delight.
Red sky in the morning, shepherd take warning.

The thought struck a rather ominous note, making her stir restlessly.

Did this dawn contain a warning to her, then? Was it possible that some danger lurked in the coming days, like the red sky in the distance? After all, she had given herself up to the night of passion so completely that she had never even paused to consider the future.

'Lucas—' she began uneasily, but he silenced her with a firm shake of his head.

'It's all right, Gia, I can manage,' he said, clearly misinterpreting the reason for her concern. 'And we'll be quicker this way. But you'd better keep quiet now. We're getting near the house and we don't want to wake anyone.'

A rumble of laughter shook the broad chest against which her head rested.

'Explanations could be a little difficult.'

The prospect alone was enough to keep Georgia silent as she lay in his arms. Looking back over his shoulder, she could see how a single trail of footsteps in the wet grass left the only evidence of the fact that they had ever been there, that the night they had shared had ever existed.

Somehow they made it back to the house and up the stairs without meeting anyone. Lucas carried her to her room and laid her gently on the bed, still wrapped tightly in the blanket.

'Try and get some sleep,' he told her softly. 'No one will think it strange if you have a lie-in after the party. I'll keep your father occupied for a couple of hours at least.'

A warm kiss, delicate as a butterfly's touch and heartbreakingly brief, brushed over her forehead and she felt him smile.

'We'll leave when you're ready.'

It was hard to fight off the waves of sleep that were threatening to engulf her, but something was nagging at her clouded brain, something that had to be said.

'Lucas, we need to talk.'

His sigh was almost silent, but she caught it.

'If we must. But later—in the car. Sleep now.'

Georgia's heavy eyes were closing, so that she didn't hear him go, but the sound of the door shutting behind him jerked her close to the surface of consciousness for a moment.

'Explanations could be a little difficult.' Lucas's voice echoed inside her head, his determination to make sure that no one found out that they had spent the night together suddenly acquiring new and disturbing undertones. Inside her head his laughing comment was overlaid by Kelly's unhappy tones.

'Mallory's Moppets...*I* barely had a chance to warm his sheets before he pushed me out the door. The proverbial one-night stand, that's me!''

The proverbial one-night stand. Was that all that she too was destined to be? 'We need to talk'—'If we must...'

She could no longer hold out against the exhaustion

that was claiming her, but even as she gave up the struggle and slid into oblivion the final image in her mind was the memory of those footprints left in the dew.

They had been Lucas's prints alone, leading away from the summerhouse and all that had happened there, and that fact now seemed to have gained a new and worryingly ominous significance.

'I thought we'd never get away!'

Lucas swung the car out of the drive and onto the main road with a sigh of relief that seemed to Georgia's over-sensitive ears to be just a little too heartfelt for her peace of mind.

Already, she felt, his mind was moving ahead, back to London, away from the time they had spent in Yorkshire. And was he also wanting to get away from the night of passion they had shared together?

'Well, if you will provide my father with his ultimate fantasy car, you have only yourself to blame if he isn't exactly willing to let it go.'

Her voice sounded revealingly tart, and clearly Lucas thought so too, if the swift, frowning, sidelong glance he threw at her was anything to go by. But he made no comment, simply nodding towards the clock on the dashboard.

'Well, it doesn't matter now. We should be able to make up lost time on the motorway, and still hope to reach London by early evening.'

'Why the hurry?' Georgia couldn't hold back the question, his eagerness stabbing at her sharply.

'I have an appointment this evening.'

'And is this appointment business or pleasure?' Her acid tone earned her another sharp frown, but Lucas answered evenly enough.

'Well, it certainly doesn't come under the heading of work.'

'Pleasure, then,' Georgia deduced. 'And obviously it's

with someone very important, seeing as you're in such a rush.'

'Yes, Lyndsay is important.'

Lyndsay! The woman's name twisted the knife that suspicion had already pushed deep into a raw wound in her heart. Although those dreadful words 'one-night stand' and the ominous possibilities implied by them had crept into her mind earlier, she had refused to let them take root. She hadn't wanted to consider the fact that that might be all she had been to Lucas.

But now his anxiety to get back to this Lyndsay meant that she was forced to face up to the unpleasant truths she had dodged earlier.

'And of course you've fully discharged your commitment to me. There's no further obligation on your part. After all, I'm not paying you for today.'

'Don't be stupid, Gia! This has nothing to do with money.'

Lucas negotiated the roundabout that led onto the motorway, waiting until they were once more speeding in a straight line before speaking again.

'Just what's got into you? Are you still smarting from what your dad said as we left?'

'Not at all!'

Perhaps in the past her father's farewell, his final comment of, 'I always said you should have been a boy,' might have stung bitterly, but today her mind had been on other things.

'If you must know, I actually took it as something of a compliment,' she managed with a touch of defiance, and was frankly surprised when Lucas smiled and nodded agreement.

'So did I. I rather suspect that, deep down, your papa is far more proud of you than he will ever admit. He just can't bring himself to say so. One thing I've been wondering—is his attitude the reason why you're still single? Because—?'

'Because I never met a man who matched up to my father's exacting standards, is that what you mean?'

'Who confirmed his bigoted prejudices is more like it!' Lucas retorted. 'After all, any man you met would hardly stand a chance. If they weren't your father's type they'd never be a match for you, and if they were—'

'They'd be the sort who simply moved in and tried to take over,' Georgia put in feelingly. 'I've had plenty of experience of *them*!'

And Lucas was another one, she told herself bitterly, though in a rather different way. He was someone who, while appearing to do as she wanted, had in fact been manipulating the situation all the time, taking it out of her hands and turning it into just what *he* wanted.

'And is that how you see me, Gia?'

The sharpness of Lucas's intuition tightened Georgia's nerves so that she stiffened in her seat, wondering if he could actually probe deep into her mind and read her thoughts.

'After all, you said that I reminded you of your father. Do you think of me simply as some sort of chauvinistic macho type who fits into Ben Harding's narrow definition of male?'

'It's how I *saw* you.'

How she wished she could deny it, but if she did she wouldn't be telling the truth. Because wasn't that exactly how she had seen him at first, and precisely what she had wanted from him?

And now? She had no answer to that question, even for herself. As she had got to know Lucas better she had discovered other, very different sides to him. But she had no idea which Lucas Mallory had been with her last night—or rather, early this morning.

'How you saw me,' Lucas echoed ominously. 'And now?'

If she had been unable to answer when she had asked herself that question, then she was even less capable of responding to it now, particularly when it was put to her in that dangerously quiet tone.

'What makes you think anything has changed?'

She aimed to sound challenging, but couldn't quite iron out the quaver in her voice that came from a deep inner awareness of just how much had changed. Lucas was no longer just a man she had met, the man whose services she had bid for at the auction, whom she had paid to act as her escort at the party. He was the man she loved, and that changed everything.

'I see. In that case, why did you sleep with me?'

Because I couldn't help myself; because I would have died if I hadn't. But why did *you* sleep with me?

'Because I wanted to!' She hid her fear behind a veneer of ice. 'Because you are one hell of a sexy guy, as I'm sure you know only too well. I mean, to quote my friend, Kelly, what woman in her right mind would turn down the chance of a night with Lucas Mallory, the fastest man on the track?'

'Kelly—'

Lucas pounced on the name like a hunting cat on a sluggish mouse.

'Your friend, Kelly. Would that be the friend who was so eloquent about my reputation? Who was so quick to point out how well I deserved it?'

Georgia wished she could go back in time to a point just a few minutes earlier, so that she could bite on her tongue to hold back the too-revealing name. But it was too late for that now, and she could only nod in apprehensive silence.

'And would that Kelly be Kelly Preston?'

'So you do remember individual conquests!'

A twist of distress at the way he had made no attempt to deny Kelly's accusations, the fact that he recalled her name seeming to confirm all her friend had said, pushed her into cattiness.

'I certainly remember my time with dear Kelly. It's not an encounter I'm likely to forget.'

'So it was true.'

Even now, some weak part of her heart had foolishly hoped that Kelly's story had been exaggerated or inaccurate in some way, and she hated him for confirming the sordid details.

'She said you couldn't wait to get rid of her. How could you be so callous, so careless of her feelings?'

Lucas's indifferent shrug dismissed her comments, and Kelly along with them.

'Believe me, she asked for everything she got.'

And he couldn't care less about the way she had felt.

'So what about me?' The question escaped before she had a chance to consider the wisdom of asking it.

'You? What about you?'

'Am I any different from Kelly, and all the others in your past?'

'Do you want to be different?' Lucas asked coldly, not taking his eyes from the road.

'Don't fence with me! You know what I mean.'

'Do I?'

Suddenly, without warning, Lucas swung the car into the feed-in lane that led to the motorway services, speeding into the almost empty car park and ramming on the brakes with scant regard for the Morgan's expensive engine. They had barely come to a halt before he rounded on her, dangerous fires blazing in the depths of his eyes.

'If you mean do I intend to become just a trophy husband, marrying you so that you can flaunt me in front of your father, use me as a way to win his approval for ever, then, no, I have no intention of being trapped in that way!'

'I never—' Georgia began indignantly, then broke off, her conscience distinctly uncomfortable as she recalled the scene in the conservatory the night before. She had to admit to her own weak thoughts, even if they'd lasted only for a few seconds.

'Never?' Lucas's question was darkly sardonic. 'Are you telling me that it never crossed your mind?'

'I— That was never how I saw you.' Lucas could never be anyone's trophy; never *just* anything!

But she had hesitated too long; her silence betrayed her.

'You'll have to forgive me if I don't exactly believe you.' The bite in the words made it plain that an apology was the furthest thing from his mind. 'And I'm sorry, but I really don't fancy putting my head into that particular noose.'

'No one asked you to! After all, no one but a fool would want a man with your reputation—!'

'Reputation!' Lucas cut in savagely. 'So we're back to that again, are we, darling? And all on dear Kelly's say-so, I presume. So tell me, sweet Gia, if I'm such a terrible womaniser—a callous heartbreaker who woos naïve young innocents and then tosses them aside without a second thought—if your opinion of me is so appallingly low, then why am I here with you? Why did you ever choose me in the first place?'

'Perhaps that's exactly why!' The need to hide her pain gave her voice a strength she hadn't thought possible. 'Because with someone like you there would be no danger of any sort of emotional involvement.'

At least, not on *his* part, her mind threw at her, and she was stabbed to the heart with the pain of the thought. She had done everything she could to guarantee no complications of that sort where Lucas was concerned, but she had never considered the possibility of them ruining things for *her*. Knowing that made her want to lash out, to hurt him as she was hurting.

'I would just use you as you used all those others.'

'So that's it! This is some sort of twisted revenge fantasy. You see yourself as some wonderful avenging

angel out to punish the sinful male for all the wrongs he
has dared to inflict on the rest of womankind!'

'Oh, now you're just being ridiculous!' Georgia
laughed in scorn. 'The idea is tempting, but I'm afraid
that my motives were nothing like as idealistic as you
describe. I told you: I simply wanted your services for
twenty-four hours.'

'Exactly,' Lucas put in harshly. 'You bought me for
twenty-four hours. Midnight to midnight. And I gave
you value for money—the best!'

He laced the words with a dark cynicism which had
Georgia flinching back in her seat.

'But the arrangement was for that one day, nothing
more.'

She had always known it, Georgia told herself miserably; she should have expected this. Hadn't Kelly
warned her? And even Lucas himself had had the honesty not to deny the truth of what he was really like.

But all the same she was unprepared for such a blunt
declaration of the facts. Her heart was totally unpro-
tected, far too vulnerable to the blow that made it feel
as if it had been torn into tiny pieces.

'That was all I ever wanted.' She made herself say it,
even though the real cost of all that had happened was
etched into her soul in letters of blood. 'And I have to
agree, you certainly gave value for money.'

The black scowl that crossed his face terrified her so
that she shrank back against the car door.

'Do you know?' he said in a voice that froze her
blood, each word falling on her skin like drops of ice.
'Until this moment I never really understood why you
ever acquired the nickname of Ice Maiden, but now I
do. Now I see only too clearly.'

And now, just when she thought that she had faced
all there was to face, his words put a new and even more
devastating fear into Georgia's mind. She'd forgotten he
knew about that hateful nickname. Was it possible that,

as with others in the past, that description of her character had been in his mind all along?

'Is that how you saw it?' she demanded. 'Was the idea of the Ice Maiden a challenge to your masculine ego, to that one hundred percent record on which you built your *reputation*? Did you set out to prove that you—the great Lucas Mallory—were the one who could—who could...'

'Make the Ice Maiden melt once and for all?' Lucas finished for her when she couldn't bring herself to say the words. 'Well, if that was the case then last night certainly proved a point. You're no more an Ice Maiden, my darling Gia, than I'm any sort of a saint. In my arms you were all fire and heat, burning up with the sort of passion that a man only encounters on very rare occasions, if he's lucky. You were as wild and elemental as the storm outside. You surely aren't going to try to deny that!'

She would have given the world to be able to do so, but she knew there was no hope of getting away with any such thing. The only fact she prayed she could hide from him was the reason *why* she had responded so openly, so passionately. If she could do nothing else, then at least she could protect herself from his ever finding out that she loved him.

'And last night?' It was impossible to keep the bitterness from her voice. 'Was that too part of your services rendered? Was it included in the price, or can I expect a bill in due course?'

'Oh, no, sweetheart, that was an extra, and it came absolutely free, no charge at all. Why do you ask?'

A wicked smile curled that sensually wide mouth, making Georgia think unwillingly of the serpent in the garden of Eden, deliberately setting out to tempt Eve.

'Were you wondering if you could afford me again?'

Leaning forward slowly, he lifted one hand, letting his fingers trail down the side of her cheek, his dark eyes holding hers hypnotically, clearly noting her uncontrollable shiver of response as his smile widened.

'Do you want to do it again?' he murmured, his voice smokily seductive. 'Would you—?'

'No, I would *not*!' Georgia repulsed his caress with a violent movement of her head. 'I don't want anything to do with you in any way whatsoever! Never, ever again! I have no intention of becoming anything so demeaning as one of Mallory's Moppets!'

That had hit home. Lucas's head went back sharply, his eyes narrowing to mere slits in a face where the skin was drawn so taut over his strong cheekbones that white lines of anger were etched around his nose and mouth.

'That wasn't what I had in mind!' he snarled. 'You weren't asked—'

'Well, even if I had been, the answer would have been a very definite *no*!'

'As it was last night?' Lucas queried with hateful mockery.

'Last night was a mistake! The biggest mistake of my life.'

'And mine!' Lucas flung at her, destroying her control completely.

'Oh, God, I hate you! I never want to see you again in my life!'

'A little difficult, darling, seeing as we still have over a hundred miles to travel together. Even if I break the speed limit, I reckon you'll have to endure at least another couple of hours.'

The thought was more than she could bear.

'No way! I'll make my own way from here—get a bus or a train.' She was fumbling with the doorhandle as she spoke, unnerved to find it locked. 'Let me out of here!'

'Gia, don't be bloody stupid!'

The harsh-toned use of his own private name for her was positively the last straw. He had used that name the previous night in a voice husky with passion, with an emotion she had been fool enough to allow herself to believe in.

'I'd be more stupid to stay in this car with you any longer than I had to! If you don't let me out, I shall scream. And *don't* call me Gia. My name is Georgia. Now, *open this door!*'

What was frightening was the complete lack of emotion with which he did as she demanded, moving to release the catch with a vicious movement, his face set into such cold, hard lines that it looked as if it was carved from a block of ice.

Grabbing her handbag, Georgia scrambled out of the car, landing inelegantly on the tarmac and slamming the door hard behind her.

It had barely closed before Lucas rammed his foot down hard on the accelerator and jolted the car into movement. He swung it away from her at a rate that set the engine roaring and made her heart leap into her throat in fear, even though she knew that, to Lucas, it was probably only a sedate crawl when compared to the record-breaking speeds he had reached on the race track.

What sort of fool was she? she asked herself as the Morgan disappeared from view. Was it possible that, even after the way he had treated her, the appalling things he had said, she still cared what happened to him? But she loved him, and, crazy as it was, nothing had happened to change that.

It was only then that she realised she had left her overnight bag in the car, still safely stowed in the Morgan's boot.

The thought of the dress that Lucas had chosen for her, the earrings he had given her before the party brought back the memory of how she had felt then. She had let herself dream but it had been just a foolish idyll, a bubble of fantasy with which she had surrounded herself, forgetting reality for that short space of time.

Well, now that bubble had well and truly burst, and cold, harsh reality was hitting her hard in the face, so that at last she had to see the truth for what it was. And the true fact was that she could never ever get the dream back again.

CHAPTER ELEVEN

'GEORGIE, you look dreadful. Don't tell me that *you're* going down with this wretched flu now.'

'I don't think so.' Georgia kept her gaze fixed on her desk in order to avoid Kelly's eyes. 'I'm just tired. I haven't been sleeping very well.'

Understatement of the year, her mind threw at her. She doubted if she'd had a full night's sleep in total since the appalling weekend of her father's birthday, now over two weeks ago.

And what rest she had managed had been disturbed by haunting, erotic images of Lucas as he had appeared on that night in the summerhouse. She had seen once again his strong body bathed in the pale moonlight, his eyes deep, bottomless pools. She had heard his huskily soft voice promising sensual delights in a way that had her writhing in heated response, struggling to break free from the hold that the dream had on her.

Forcing herself awake, she had been horrified to find that the need his words had woken in her had not been just part of the fantasy. Instead it was a gnawing, aching reality that lingered unappeased, driving her to distraction as her restless body demanded a satisfaction it had been denied.

'And there's been a lot of extra work while you've been off,' she said now.

'It's more than that,' Kelly said in concern. 'I've never seen you like this. In fact, you haven't been yourself since that weekend you spent in Yorkshire. Georgie...'

Georgia almost groaned aloud as she saw the way her friend's mind was working.

'Did something go wrong then?'

'You could say that.'

'With your dad?'

Clearly, Georgia's expression gave her an answer without any words needing to be spoken, because Kelly gave a groan.

'You and Lucas Mallory? I heard you were—'

'Not any more,' Georgia put in hastily, not wanting to hear those emotive words 'a couple'.

'Can I ask why not?' There was an odd note in Kelly's voice.

'Oh, Kelly, you don't really need me to answer that, do you? I really should have listened when you told me what he was like.'

'Oh, God!' Kelly had lost colour, her hand going to her mouth. 'You didn't? Oh, Georgie, I'm *sorry*!'

'It doesn't matter.'

'No, you don't understand. I mean I'm sorry I didn't exactly tell you the truth about Lucas.'

'You didn't?' Georgia felt as if some ominous note of warning was sounding in her head, setting her nerves on edge. 'So what *exactly* is the truth?'

'Oh, dear.' Her friend looked painfully shamefaced. 'I did meet him at a nightclub, like I said. He chatted for a while, bought me a drink. He didn't know I'd already had more than I could really handle, and I got rather drunk. Lucas took me home and I—I—'

Fiery colour flooded the younger girl's cheeks, leaving Georgia in no doubt as to just what had happened.

'You propositioned him?'

Kelly nodded, her eyes dark with embarrassment.

'I threw myself at him—told him I was his to do with as he pleased.'

'And he took advantage of the fact that you were drunk—!' It was worse than she'd thought.

'No, Georgie,' Kelly broke in hastily. 'It wasn't like
that at all. He didn't do *anything*. Well, unless you call
"anything" giving me the dressing down of my life and
calling me every sort of fool possible before walking out
and leaving me to realise just what an idiot I'd been.'

'And that's *all*?'

A miserable nod gave her her answer. 'Honest,
Georgie, I made up all the rest.'

Georgia felt as if her head was spinning sickeningly.
In her thoughts she could hear Lucas's hard declaration,
'she asked for everything she got,' her heart quailing at
the thought of the erroneous interpretation she had put
on that.

'But why?'

Her friend sighed, her colour growing deeper by the
second.

'I really don't feel good about this, Georgie, but you
see, that night I'd boasted to the others I was with that
I'd get Lucas Mallory to notice me. That's why I made
a play for him, and so many people saw us leave together
they really thought I'd cracked it. The next day they all
wanted to know what had happened; what he'd been
like.'

That Georgia could well believe. Hadn't she been subjected to something of the sort after she'd 'bought'
Lucas at the auction?

'I just couldn't face admitting that he hadn't been in
the least bit interested in me, that he'd just seen me home
out of a sense of responsibility because he'd realised I
wasn't exactly sober. I mean, how would you feel if you
were the only woman Lucas Mallory *wasn't* interested
in?'

'So you lied.' Georgia's tone was hollow, her thoughts
elsewhere. She was thinking back over that last day with
Lucas, the argument in the car on their journey to
London.

'I'm afraid so. I was sure that I'd never see him again,

and there'd been so many women linked with him over the years. What harm could one more name on the list do? It's not as if he had any reputation to lose.'

Georgia winced away from the bitter power of that word 'reputation'.

'So I embroidered on the truth, let people think I'd been just a one-night stand, and they swallowed it.' Her face was as full of remorse as her tone. 'You swallowed it.'

'I swallowed it,' Georgia echoed flatly, knowing that she had swallowed Kelly's story hook, line and sinker, and that it had prejudiced her view of Lucas right from the start.

And would it have made things any different if she *had* known the truth? Or was it a fact that she had found Kelly's story only too easy to accept because she was already predisposed to that way of thinking? With her view of men already darkened by her father's attitude, and the feeling reinforced by Jason's behaviour, she had been only too ready to believe it.

And wasn't it because she had been so ready to believe that she had chosen Lucas in the first place? Believing him to be heartless, had she set out to use him in exactly the way that he had accused her of doing?

'And now I've messed things up for you.'

'No,' Georgia admitted with bitter honesty. 'I was more than capable of messing it up for myself.'

'Perhaps if I rang him, told him…?'

'No! If anyone tells him, it should be me.'

But would he even listen? Wouldn't she be just as guilty of fantasising as Kelly if she let herself hope for that? After all, Kelly's story wasn't all of it.

'Kelly, I don't suppose you know of some friend of Lucas's called Lyndsay?'

'Lyndsay? No, sorry. It rings no bells.'

No, she hadn't really supposed it would. It would have

been too good to be true to have all her problems solved at one go. Life just wasn't like that.

So now what? Georgia asked herself when, after apologising for perhaps the thousandth time, Kelly finally left. Was she going to do anything about what her friend had told her, or was it better to leave things as they were?

After all, Lucas had never given any indication that he wanted anything more than a brief affair. He had said as much to her. It might have lasted rather more than the one-night stand she had believed it to be, but in the end she would still have been one of Mallory's Moppets.

'That wasn't what I had in mind!' Lucas's voice came back to haunt her. What *had* he had in mind? She hadn't given him a chance to tell her.

But she still couldn't make up her mind to take any action, and the problem remained unresolved until later that day when, while making a purchase in the local chemist's, Georgia heard her name called and spun round in surprised response.

'It is Georgia, isn't it?'

It took her a couple of seconds to recognise the elegant brunette from the boutique where Lucas had bought her the dress as the casually dressed woman with a small daughter in a pushchair.

'Vanessa! How are you?'

'I'm fine.' To Georgia's surprise, the other woman's eyes were cool, her tone of voice distant. 'Which is more than I can say for Lucas.'

'Lucas?' Georgia's heart lurched in painful apprehension. 'Why, what's wrong? Is he ill?'

'Not ill—yet. But I'm worried that he'll make himself unwell if he goes on the way he's doing. Don't you care that he's driving himself into the ground, working too hard—?'

'I'm sorry,' Georgia interrupted carefully. 'But I'm

afraid I don't see quite what this has to do with me. It isn't my fault.'

'Well, it's hardly because of anyone else!' Vanessa retorted sharply. 'You were the only woman in his life, and anyone with eyes in their head could see how that made him feel. But then, when he came to Lyndsay's party—'

'Lyndsay!' Georgia echoed the other woman's name flatly. How could Vanessa claim *Georgia* was the only woman in Lucas's life, and in the same breath mention this other one? 'You were at Lyndsay's party?'

And that party must have been the reason why Lucas had been so impatient to get back to London, his concern to be on time just the thin end of the wedge that had finally come between them.

'Well, of course I was.' Vanessa looked frankly taken aback. 'I would hardly miss my own daughter's birthday celebrations!'

'Daughter!'

Georgia's shadowed hazel eyes went to the little girl in the pushchair, receiving a beaming grin that made her heart turn over inside her. '*This* is Lyndsay?'

Vanessa nodded agreement. 'My daughter, Lucas's godchild. She was two a fortnight ago—the day after your trip to Yorkshire, in fact. Lucas promised that whatever happened he'd be at her party. He didn't explain?'

She hadn't given him a chance to do so, Georgia admitted miserably. Already prejudiced against him, and with Kelly's fabricated story in her mind, she'd reacted exactly as he had accused her of doing. She had tried and convicted him without waiting for any evidence for the defence.

'I really thought you cared for him. That day when you came to my shop—'

'But that was…'

Georgia's voice faded as a memory struck home. She had been about to say that that had been just a business arrangement, that Lucas had only been with her because of the money she had paid at the auction, but now, recalling Lucas's face when he had first seen her in the cream dress, she was forced to wonder.

He had only agreed to act as her *escort*. There had been no need at all to help her in the way that he had, or buy the dress. And there had been nothing business-like about the way he had looked at her in Vanessa's shop, or later, on the night of the party.

The man who had made love to her in the summer-house was not the 'strictly business' partner she had demanded, but someone who, by his own declaration, had abandoned their original agreement.

Midnight to midnight, he had said, and the moment twelve o'clock had struck, he had changed all the rules.

'You might be right, Vanessa,' she said slowly, praying with all her heart that it might be so. 'I'll have to talk to Lucas.'

But would he listen? Even as she admitted to a sense of despair, sudden inspiration struck.

'I'll make him listen!' she declared. 'And seeing Lyndsay has given me an idea as to how to get through to him.'

Georgia pressed her finger on the bell of Lucas's house, knowing that never before in her life had she ever felt so desperately nervous, so afraid of all that could possibly go wrong. Her heart seemed to be beating high up in her throat, making it difficult to breathe properly, and her fingers felt damp and slippery on the handle of the briefcase she carried.

Her bank manager had been horrified at the request she had made, she recalled with a wry smile. He had wasted precious time trying to talk her out of it, but she had assured him that she had no intention of being dissuaded, and that it would all be worth it in the end.

At least, she hoped it would be, she told herself, the

knotted nerves in her stomach tightening painfully as the door swung open at last.

'Georgia.'

Lucas's tone could not have been more unwelcoming, and the hard-voiced use of her full name was totally discouraging. But *had* there been some flash of response in those dark eyes before the heavy lids had hooded them? Or was she just deceiving herself, indulging in foolish wish-fulfilment?

Certainly the shadows on his face, the lines of tiredness around his eyes and mouth, seemed to indicate that there had been some degree of truth in Vanessa's story. For now she would pin all her hopes on that. It was all she had.

'I've come to—'

'Oh, I know what you've come for.' His cold, clipped tones clashed with her own uncertain beginning, making her break off in confusion.

'You do?'

Lucas nodded, no trace of warmth or understanding lightening the obdurate set of his features. 'I have something of yours.'

Only my heart. Georgia almost blurted out the words aloud, then belated realisation set in with the memory of the overnight bag she had left in his car two weeks before and had forgotten about until now.

'I have it here.'

When he moved into a room that opened off the hallway, Georgia took her courage in both hands and followed him, not waiting to be invited in. For one thing she was sure that Lucas would never do so, and for another she was afraid her nerve would fail if she didn't act now. It was as Lucas turned, with her bag in his hands, that something started to puzzle her.

'Why didn't you just send it round to my house? I would have paid for the taxi or whatever.'

'I never thought of it.' His casual tone hurt more than

any overt hostility, implying supreme indifference to anything concerning her. 'I just dumped it in here that night when I got back and took off again. I was already late for Lyndsay's party.'

'Oh yes, Lyndsay…' Georgia snatched at the opening he had given her. 'Why didn't you tell me she was Vanessa's daughter?'

'Why didn't you ask?' Lucas countered coldly. 'Now you've got your property, so if you don't mind I—'

'Well, actually I *do* mind.'

It took all her courage to say it in the face of the cold-eyed hostility he turned on her, rejection stamped into every line of his face.

'And I have something for you.'

'I doubt if I would want anything you—'

'Well, all right!' Georgia couldn't let him finish. 'I don't suppose you do want anything from me, but this isn't for *you* exactly. I mean…'

Her attempt at explanation foundered in the face of his evident resistance, making her feel as if she was beating her head hard against a brick wall. Except that in this case it still hurt even when she stopped.

'You're not making any sense, Georgia,' Lucas drawled coolly. 'Do you really have something to say? Because if you do, I would prefer you to get on with it and then leave.'

The carefully controlled reasonableness of his tone was the last straw, and, determined to do something—anything—to break down that rigid self-restraint, Georgia swung her briefcase up on to the table, slamming it onto the polished surface and snapping open the locks.

'*This* is for that precious charity of yours!' she declared, flinging back the lid. 'For the special baby unit—all of it. If…'

Once more words failed her, and Lucas surveyed the

rows of neatly stacked banknotes, all banded together in hundred-pound bundles.

'If…' he said slowly, then suddenly the dark eyes were on her face, narrowing in hostile scrutiny. 'It's a very generous donation, but there seem to be conditions. If what, Georgia?'

Georgia. His way of saying her full name almost destroyed her, but she forced herself to go on.

'I've done some calculations, so I know what's needed.' She was gabbling in her haste to get the words out. 'Considering how much I paid for twenty-four hours with you, I've worked out an hourly rate. You said you'd do anything for the charity and—'

'What do I have to do to earn it?'

She'd thought he would never ask!

'Just *listen*! I don't want a full day this time, just long enough to let me explain.'

His silence as she finished was terrifying, stretching every nerve to near breaking point. Her teeth dug into her bottom lip as she waited, and she let the small physical pain distract her from the possibility of the appalling emotional anguish if he refused. Then at last, slowly and reluctantly, it seemed, Lucas nodded.

'All right. What did you want to talk about?'

For an appalling couple of seconds, all rational thought deserted Georgia. She had the chance she had prayed for and she must be careful not to blow it. But she didn't know where to begin or what words to use. Drawing on all her strength, she forced herself to begin.

'I've been talking to Kelly Preston— Oh, please, don't look like that! I know now that she was lying about you. She admitted she made it all up.'

'You believed it,' Lucas pointed out with icy precision.

Georgia winced away from the freezing calm of that comment. This wasn't going to be easy, but perhaps the fact that he was so absolutely determined to be hostile told its own story. Why put up defences if you felt there was nothing you needed protection against?

'Yes, I did, but I didn't know you then. And let me tell you about James.'

'James?' She had his attention now, though it wasn't a comfortable feeling to have those steely grey eyes probing deep into hers. 'Not the charmer who labelled you the Ice Maiden?'

The contemptuous description gave her something to hope for as she shook her head.

'No, James was before that, when I first came to London. I fell for him heavily, and I thought he felt the same about me. I even started thinking about marriage and a future, but...'

'He dumped you?' Lucas put in when she hesitated, and from his use of that particular phrase she knew he was thinking of the conversation they'd had about past relationships on the first night he had come to her house.

Georgia nodded, her expression sombre.

'Oh, he would have married me if I'd been prepared to adjust to how he wanted his wife to be. If I'd given up my job, agreed to become a stay-at-home wife.'

'Everything your papa wanted you to be.'

'Exactly. That was when I realised that he didn't want *me*, but some personal ideal of what he thought a woman should be like.'

'Poor Gia, first your father, then this idiot—and of course the wonderful Jason.'

Lucas's voice was soft, and even though Georgia hunted for a thread of mockery in it, she couldn't find one.

'No wonder you thought that all men just wanted to move in and take over.'

'So I concentrated my energies on my career instead.'

'And got labelled the Ice Maiden.'

Georgia's breath caught sharply in her throat because it was said with a tiny hint of a smile, the first sign of

any degree of warmth he had shown since the moment
he had opened the door to her.

'I could cope with that,' she admitted. 'It was so much
easier to stick to strictly business—until you came
along.'

The faint jerk of his head betrayed him. Perhaps anyone else might have missed the involuntary movement,
but, sensitive as she was to everything about him,
Georgia caught it, together with the swift narrowing of
his eyes.

'It wasn't so easy to be businesslike then.'

One dark eyebrow lifted in that familiar questioning
gesture.

'You certainly didn't seem to have any trouble.'

'Then I'm a far better actress than I ever realised,
because it was almost impossible to stick to my policy
with you. And you wouldn't play by the rules.'

'I didn't see any point to them,' Lucas admitted, taking her breath away. 'I'll be honest, I thought you were
some sort of control freak, someone who wanted to be
able to dictate terms.'

Suddenly he swung round to the table, strong hands
resting on the edge of the open briefcase. His dark eyes
were hooded, hiding his thoughts from her as he studied
the contents.

'There's one hell of a lot of money in here.'

'Every last penny from my savings account.' Georgia
had to choke the words out, her throat closing up over
them as those ebony eyes swung round to fix on her face
once more.

'It was worth that much?'

There was no going back now. She had to tell him
the whole truth; nothing else would do. He would know
if she held back.

'All that, and more,' she told him huskily. 'I'd have
done anything to get you to listen.'

'But why?'

'Because I made a terrible mistake when I let Kelly's story influence me instead of listening to my heart. I should have known that it wasn't as she said.'

'I don't have a very good reputation with women,' Lucas said in a very different tone of voice. 'Or rather, I used to have a very bad one.'

'Used to?' Georgia prompted when he paused, frowning down at his hands.

Suddenly Lucas's dark head came up again, and he raked his fingers roughly through the sleek darkness of his hair, looking amazingly vulnerable in a way that she had never seen before.

'Let me explain,' he said. 'I told you that my mother died when I was six. My father brought me up from then on, and really we were just like two kids instead of parent and child. We were both machine-and speed-crazy. We were totally irresponsible because there was no one there to be hurt by what we did. There was no wife to worry if he came home late, no mother to panic if I drove too fast. And I'll admit that I had the same attitude in my personal life.'

He sighed faintly, shook his dark head at his memories.

'I'd never learned to consider a woman's feelings. I'm not proud to admit that for a long time women were just something on the edges of my life—appealing enough, but very much secondary to my career.'

A wry smile touched his lips at her swiftly indrawn breath.

'Yeah, I reckon we were very much alike. But then four things happened in quick succession that changed things. Firstly my father married again, and I saw how it hurt my stepmother when he behaved as he had done in the old days, how she worried for him and about him—and me. And then Tony died.'

'And then your own crash?' Georgia put in when he

fell silent, apparently absorbed in his thoughts. Lucas nodded slowly.

'I'd seen how Nessa grieved for Tony—she was devastated—and I suddenly realised that if I had died in that crash no one would have mourned for me as she did for him.'

If he had died. Georgia couldn't suppress a fearful shudder.

'Oh, don't! Don't talk like that!'

'It was true.'

'You said four things,' Georgia prompted when once again he paused. 'What was the last one?'

Those dark eyes were deep, deep pools as they fixed on her face.

'I think you know,' Lucas said with soft intensity.

She didn't dare to hope, terrified of being wrong.

'Why don't you tell my why you're here? The real reason, not the excuse of a donation to charity.'

She wanted to so much, but didn't know if she dared. What if she opened her heart to him, only to have him fling it back in her face?

But Lucas had seen the look in her eyes and he smiled softly.

'All right.' His voice was as gentle as the hand that took hold of hers, strong fingers weaving between her more delicate ones. 'I'll make it easy for you, shall I? The fourth thing that happened, Gia, was that I met you. I met the most beautiful woman I'd ever seen, and I lost my head completely. But all she wanted from me was some emotionless business arrangement.'

His tone made it plain just what he thought of that.

'I'm sorry,' Georgia murmured, and his fingers tightened on hers.

'I realise now that you were just plain scared, but it came across as coldness—the Ice Maiden personified. I thought you were pushing me away, and so I vowed to keep my distance, keep well away.'

A wry grin surfaced again, boyishly appealing.

'I told myself I'd play it by your rules but I couldn't stay away, and when I was with you I couldn't keep my hands to myself, which was obviously not what you wanted. It seemed that all you *did* want was someone who could impress your dad, so I decided I'd do that, and then maybe, in time...'

'You did more than that,' Georgia put in hastily. 'The things you said to my father...'

'I meant every word. Remember, I promised you that I'd only say things I really meant, and when I realised how much I did mean them I knew I was lost. I knew that I loved you.'

'Loved!' Georgia cried. 'Oh, God, Lucas, I accused you of wanting to make me—'

'One of those damned Moppets! God, Gia, if you only knew what you put me through that day, storming off like that. Nessa nearly killed me when I finally arrived too late for the party.'

'Too late? But—' Realisation dawned as she looked into his face. 'You didn't just drive off!'

'And leave you alone in a strange place?' Lucas looked horrified at the thought. 'I *couldn't*. I waited around out of sight until you got a taxi, then I followed it from the services to the station. Only when I knew you were safely on a train did I set off for London. I broke all my old track records on the way, but I was still late.'

Lucas shook his dark head in despair at the memory.

'I had planned to use the time on that journey to tell you how I really felt. I wanted to ask you if you thought we had any hope of a future. Instead, I ended up driving you out of the car and then following you from a distance like some private detective in a Raymond Chandler novel. The only thing that gave me any hope was that I still had your bag, and I knew that if I hung on to it at some point you'd have to come round to collect it.'

'Which I did.'

'Yes, but I hadn't anticipated your offering me a fortune in used notes as well! So now, Gia, are you still so afraid, or can you tell me what you really came to say?'

With his grey eyes on her face, his hands in hers, strong, warm and encouraging, she had all the courage she needed.

'I wanted to tell you that I love you, that I can't live without you, that...'

She got no further because Lucas's arms came round her, gathering her close as his lips came down on hers and he kissed her with such passionate thoroughness that her head was spinning when he finally released her. Still with one arm around his waist, she turned and ran a finger along the edge of the open briefcase.

'I've forgotten what the hourly rate worked out at,' she told him teasingly, her hazel eyes glowing as they looked into his. 'But do you think there's enough here to persuade you to spend the rest of your life with me?'

'More than enough,' Lucas assured her, his voice deep and husky with emotion. 'You know, you never needed to bring the money in the first place. All you had to do was ask, and I would have listened—till the end of my days, if you'd wanted. I can't resist you, can't deny you anything, my love—particularly when you turn those beautiful, pleading eyes on me.'

'Is that a fact?'

Georgia turned to look up at him, deliberately opening her eyes as wide as she could as she moved closer, resting her head against his shoulder and trailing soft fingertips along the strong lines of his chest. Her lips curved into a smile of joyful triumph as she felt the shudder of reaction that shook his strong body.

'So if I was to ask you to take me to bed right now and show me how much you love me...'

The immediate increase in the rate of his heartbeat

gave her his answer. It was there too in the darkness of
his eyes, in the way he swallowed hard.

'God, Gia,' he told her rawly, 'you don't have to ask.
There is only you for me. You and no other woman.
From the moment I set eyes on you at that damn auction
I knew that I was under your spell, and even if you
hadn't bought me that night I would still have been your
slave for life.'

Coming
Next Month...

A special promotion
from

Seduction and Passion Guaranteed!

Details to follow in September 2002
Harlequin Presents books.

Don't miss it!

The world's bestselling romance series.

HARLEQUIN®
Presents

Seduction and Passion Guaranteed!

SOCIETY WEDDINGS

**They're gorgeous, they're glamorous...
and they're getting married!**

Be our VIP guest at two of the most-talked-about
weddings of the decade—lavish ceremonies where the
cream of society gather to celebrate these marriages
in dazzling international settings.

Welcome to the sensuous, scandalous world
of the rich, royal and renowned!

SOCIETY WEDDINGS
Two original short stories in one volume:

Promised to the Sheikh
by *Sharon Kendrick*

The Duke's Secret Wife
by *Kate Walker*
on sale August, #2268

**Pick up a Harlequin Presents® novel and you will
enter a world of spine-tingling passion and
provocative, tantalizing romance!**

HARLEQUIN®
Makes any time special ®

*Available wherever
Harlequin books
are sold.*

The world's bestselling romance series.

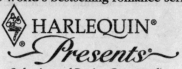

HARLEQUIN®
Presents

Seduction and Passion Guaranteed!

GREEK TYCOONS

**They're the men who have everything—
except a bride...**

Wealth, power, charm—what else could a
heart-stoppingly handsome tycoon need? In the
GREEK TYCOONS miniseries you have already
been introduced to some gorgeous Greek
multimillionaires who are in need of wives.

Bestselling author *Jacqueline Baird* presents

THE GREEK TYCOON'S REVENGE
Harlequin Presents, #2266
Available in August

Marcus had found Eloise and he wants revenge—by
making Eloise his mistress for one year!

This tycoon has met his match, and he's decided he *has* to
have her...*whatever* that takes!

**Pick up a Harlequin Presents® novel and you will
enter a world of spine-tingling passion and
provocative, tantalizing romance!**

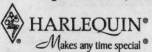

HARLEQUIN®
Makes any time special ®

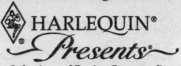